THE WRATH OF ACHILLES

FOLLOW YOUR FATES SERIES

The *Follow Your Fates* series enlists you the reader as the main character in the classic literature of ancient Greece and Rome. You assume the identity of each character, follow his story, and make the decisions he makes. Each decision you make will determine whether or not you continue to follow your fate, or whether your fate will quickly come to an end. Make the right choices and you too can complete the quests of the greatest heroes of the ancient world.

Each *Follow Your Fates* story adheres to the story of its ancient counterpart. If you successfully follow your fate, you will experience firsthand the story of the ancient original. For instance, in order to complete the full story of *The Wrath of Achilles*, you must make the decisions that Achilles makes. But do not expect these decisions to be obvious or logical. Many of these decisions in fact might seem wrong or uncomfortable by today's standards. You may find yourself making decisions that you don't agree with so that you can continue to follow your fate. These differences, however, provide an important opportunity for comparison and are the unique aspect of this series: in a more traditional format you the reader remain detached from the character and analyze his decisions objectively; you are not invested in those decisions in any way. In the *Follow Your Fates* series you yourself are making these decisions; you are forced to analyze your own motivations and reasoning. You should consider what made you make your decision and what might have made the character make his decision. In this way, you will learn not only about the ancient world and its values but also about yourself and your values.

Finally, have fun. My goal for this series is simple: to introduce readers to the literature, history, and mythology of the ancient world in an engaging, enjoyable way. Ancient literature is some of the most important in the world if for no other reason than that it has lasted so long. The reason it has lasted so long? Readers of every age and type have found something of value in it and have done so for over 2,000 years. Will the books written today last so long? We'll just have to wait and see. Until then, enjoy the classics of ancient Greece and Rome.

THE WRATH OF ACHILLES

By

ED DEHORATIUS

ILLUSTRATED BY

BRIAN DELANDRO HARDISON

Bolchazy-Carducci Publishers, Inc.
Mundelein, Illinois USA

Editor: Laurie Haight Keenan
Contributing Editor: Andrew Reinhard
Cover Design & Typography: Adam Phillip Velez
Illustrations: Brian Delandro Hardison

The Wrath of Achilles

Ed DeHoratius

Bolchazy-Carducci Publishers, Inc.
1570 Baskin Road
Mundelein, Illinois 60060
www.bolchazy.com

Printed in the United States of America
2013
by Publishers' Graphics

ISBN 978-0-86516-708-7

For Mom, who recognized and nurtured the writer in me long before I did.

Acknowledgments

First and foremost, I need to thank Christine Rhodes, Wayland High School class of 2003, whose *Choose Your Own Adventure* senior project on the Black Death showed me the potential of marrying that format with academic material and ultimately inspired the *Follow Your Fates* series. The students of the Wayland High School classes of 2007 and 2008 who took my Classical Literature class read early drafts of *The Wrath of Achilles* and provided suggestions about the text and encouragement to continue with the project. Andrew Reinhard of Bolchazy-Carducci was instrumental in bringing this project to fruition and Laurie Haight Keenan of Bolchazy-Carducci was an invaluable resource on all things editorial. Lou and Marie Bolchazy too deserve great thanks not only for their continued support and promotion of the classics but also for their willingness to experiment and take risks. As always, my family, Liz, Will, Matt, and Andrew, my parents, and the Kennedys, have shown infinite patience as I continue to write.

INTRODUCTION

A huge wooden horse towering over the walls of an ancient city. This is the enduring image of the Trojan War. The ancient Greeks had been fighting the Trojans, a people who live in the northwest corner of what is today modern Turkey, for ten years. The Trojan prince Paris had kidnapped the most beautiful woman in the world, a Greek woman named Helen. The Greeks besieged the city to get Helen back, and after ten years Troy finally fell.

The best known warrior of the Trojan War is a Greek named Achilles. He is a universal character, a warrior who cannot separate his identity on the battlefield from his identity off; he is always intense, always ready to fight, always warring. It is Achilles that you will become in *The Wrath of Achilles*. His story, as told by the Greek poet Homer in the epic poem the *Iliad*, is a brief one—of the ten years of the Trojan War, the *Iliad* covers only a few weeks. Although *The Wrath of Achilles* will go slightly beyond the scope of the *Iliad*, nonetheless you will inhabit the character of Achilles as he moves through this tumultuous and tragic three-week period as described by Homer in the *Iliad*. Make the choices that Achilles makes in the *Iliad* and you will follow your fate to a successful completion. Good luck!

THE WRATH OF ACHILLES

Your goddess mother Thetis has appeared to you as you prepare to depart for the Trojan War. She is pleading with you not to go and presents you with a choice. You can travel to Troy, be the best Greek warrior, achieve eternal glory, but die at a young age. Or you can stay home, live a long life as a farmer with only your neighbors knowing you, and die in old age.

You have a choice to make.

If you ignore your mother's pleas and continue to the Trojan War, turn to page 7.

If you listen to your mother and stay home, turn to page 19.

1

You somehow maintain your manners as you politely decline their invitation. While you wish the Greeks well, victory must be theirs without you; your honor remains insulted.

As you sit in your tent, you hear the clatter of arms as the two armies come together. You hear the cheers of the Greeks as they push the Trojans back. You hear the encouragement of Agamemnon as he urges the army forward. And you hear his men respond to his encouragement.

You realize, with a heavy heart, that the Greeks are winning without you, that they no longer need you to win. And you know that you are no longer their champion. Agamemnon has won. He has replaced you as the leader of the Greeks. Whether you stay in your tent, or sail home, it doesn't matter. The Greeks will have victory without you.

THE END

You have been at Troy for ten years and have distinguished yourself among your fellow Greeks. Indeed, every Greek knows that Achilles is the best of the Greeks and the one who will lead them to victory.

But jealousy simmers in the Greek camp, and something is about to happen that will change the course of the war and your life.

Turn to page 6.

Agamemnon smiles triumphantly as he leads your slave-girl away to his tent. You burn with anger but take comfort in your self-sacrifice. You feel satisfied because you put aside your own desires for a greater good: that of your comrades and the war. You will not let Agamemnon's foolish behavior provoke you unnecessarily.

You return to your tent, awaiting tomorrow's battle, eager to rejoin the fight with your men, even if your confidence in your leader has been shaken.

Turn to page 42.

You are a soldier. But you are not a monster. You agree to Hector's honorable pact.

The battle begins. You feel your strength surging as you bear down on the weaker Hector. But Hector is not as weak as you initially thought. He gains the upper hand and for a moment you are worried. But you remember your mother and your friend, and your strength returns.

Hector is now on the ground before you. He appears as if he is going to speak, perhaps to ask for your mercy, but he knows what your answer will be. You don't wait to see if he will ask the question. Your sword is through him as his life leaves him.

Turn to page 15.

Agamemnon, the brother of Helen's husband Menelaus and the leader of the Greek army, has angered the god Apollo. One of Apollo's priests, who is a Trojan, came to Agamemnon to beg for the return of his daughter, who had been taken as a slave in the war. Agamemnon was rude to the priest and insulted him, sending him back to Troy with nothing but ridicule. The priest prayed to Apollo to punish Agamemnon for his insolence and Apollo heard his prayer. The god began striking down the Greeks with his arrows; the Greeks could do nothing to stop their own destruction.

Finally, a Greek priest revealed to Agamemnon the solution to the plague afflicting the Greeks: Agamemnon must return the priest's daughter.

Turn to page 9.

Your mother realizes that she can not convince you to stay out of the war. She departs, and she is sad because she knows the fate that awaits you. At least she knows now that it is your choice; she will do what she can to help you in the war.

You, however, cannot linger on your mother's disappointment. You must prepare for battle.

Turn to page 3.

"Agamemnon insists that it is his right to take
your slave-girl to replace his."

Agamemnon is enraged that he must return his slave-girl. But he realizes its necessity for the success of the Greek army; he unhappily sends her back with her father.

But Agamemnon, now without a slave-girl, seeks a replacement for his own. His eyes turn to yours, whom you won in battle fair and square. Indeed, he insists that it is his right to take your slave-girl to replace his and does so without even asking your permission.

You now are the enraged one, insulted before your Greek peers. Your honor is at stake. But is your honor worth the price of the war itself? You have a choice to make.

If you choose to swallow your pride for the sake of the war and ignore Agamemnon's slight to your honor, turn to page 4.

If you choose to stand up to your leader and preserve your honor, turn to page 23.

The army cheers when they see you appear, but their joy is short-lived; they are still in the midst of a battle, and they can smell victory.

You join the battle and feel the familiar rush of adrenalin as your instincts return. Bodies fall before you, and you exalt in your choice to return.

But suddenly you hear Agamemnon's voice ringing over the Greek army: "Forward, Greeks, forward! Troy will be ours!" The army cheers as one, and troops surge past you, following Agamemnon and his call.

You soon realize that the army now looks to Agamemnon as their leader; you are simply another one of his generals, no longer the glory of the Greek army.

Your heart sinks, and your energy leaves you. You know that it no longer matters whether you continue to fight or not.

You slump on the ground as the army surges past you, and weep for the glory that will never be yours again.

THE END

You think for a moment about Patroclus' suggestion. It allows you to preserve your honor, but at the same time to help your comrades. You agree, though somewhat reluctantly.

Patroclus, now dressed in your armor, looks intimidating even to you. You realize that Patroclus' plan will work; the Greeks will push the Trojans back with Patroclus at their lead. But at the same time, you are concerned. Wearing your armor, and the success that it will inevitably bring, could be dangerous for Patroclus. If he becomes overly confident, if he begins to think that he is you and goes too far, if something should happen to him . . . that is something you couldn't live with.

You warn him, a condition for his wearing your armor: do not pursue the Trojans to the walls. Get them away from the Greek ships, but once that is accomplished, once the tide has turned, leave the fighting to the rest of the army.

He nods, but his eyes shine with a fervor that worries you.

Turn to page 40.

You motion those Greeks around you to silence. This is your moment of triumph and you will not let them ruin it. You pause in silence before speaking. "Hector was our greatest enemy. He was the Trojan hero. Now he is dead. Let us release him into the care of his people and his family. Let us not bear any further ill will toward him. I hated him for killing my friend Patroclus, but now that he is dead, I must let go of my anger. So too should you. Let Hector have the hero's funeral that he deserves. This I command."

You see in your companions' eyes disappointment and surprise. Although you are correct, these soldiers are too angry to understand your compassion. They cannot yet let go of their anger. They turn away and return to camp without a word or a look in your direction. You realize now that you can no longer lead them. They require something from their leader that you can no longer give them. You only hope that they can experience the peace of compassion in war that you have. But you fear they cannot.

THE END

The army musters on the plain between the Greek ships and the Trojan walls. The Trojans are waiting. You assume your customary place at the front of the force, your gold helmet gleaming in the sunlight, your shield ready, your sword raised.

Agamemnon gives the signal. The armies come together like thunder. Was that a snake you saw out of the corner of your eye? You pay it no heed and get swept up into the torrent of the fight.

The battle seesaws back and forth. The Trojans push the Greeks back to their ships. The momentum shifts, and the Greeks push the Trojans back almost to their walls. But you feel the Trojans surging again; you feel them winning. It has not yet happened, but you now envision the Greeks losing the war.

Continue to the next page.

"Achilles! Where are you?! We need you now!" You hear Agamemnon's voice, hoping to finish the Trojans off once and for all. But instead of inspiring you, it only makes you angry. You remember the insult, you remember the shame, and you cannot bring yourself to forgive him. You continue to fight, but you know now that it is useless. You can no longer champion the Greek cause. You pray only that you perish on the battlefield, so you don't have to live with the shame of defeat.

Soon the Trojans have regained their ground. Now the Trojans have pushed your Greeks back to their ships. And this time there is no surge from the Greeks. The acrid smell of burning wood touches your nostrils. The smoke from the burning Greek ships rises into the air. Men scream. You remain quiet. Though you may survive this battle, you know now that you will not survive the war. You continue to fight, waiting stoically for . . .

THE END

As you watch Priam, Hector's father, collect his son's body, you are strangely dissatisfied. Your anger over Patroclus' death remains, despite the death of his killer. Your heart sinks as you realize that your lust for this war is over. Whatever might happen to the rest of the Greeks, you will go home, dissatisfied, and embarrassed at your inability to avenge your friend's death. For you, this is . . .

THE END

It has been two weeks since Agamemnon insulted you. The Greeks, behind your lead, have been gaining ground on the Trojans, who seem to be weakening.

Despite your success, however, your heart has not been in the fight. You feel that much of your leadership and bravado has been manufactured. It has worked thus far, but your resolve for pretense is weakening.

You are uncertain if you can continue in this way for much longer.

If you choose to maintain your façade of bravado and continue to fight, turn to page 48.

If you choose to reassess your choices, return to page 39.

You understand immediately the look in your men's eyes: it is distrust, shaken confidence, fear, disgust. It is the same look with which you followed Agamemnon's back as he left you yesterday with your slave-girl.

His slight to your honor has done irreparable damage to your reputation in the eyes of your men. Tragically, you realize that you can no longer lead them effectively. Without a word you return to your tent and ask your squire to remove your armor.

You will leave Troy immediately and return home disgraced.

THE END

You pause for a moment, your heart softening as you think about your comrades dying and the Trojans triumphant. You meet the eyes of the men before you, and you nod slowly. They smile broadly, newly confident in the potential of the Greek army for victory. Your return will swing the tide of the battle.

After you arm yourself, you lead your men back to the body of the Greek army. Agamemnon waits for you quietly. You approach him, forcing yourself to meet his eyes; you remain angry and embarrassed. He speaks. You don't hear him. You receive his gifts stiffly and pass them along to your assistants. You take back the girl Briseis; she too goes with your assistants. Agamemnon clasps you around the back of the neck, exhorting you to inspire the Greek army to victory. The Trojans are near. The army needs their leader.

You assent aloud, but wonder silently if your heart is in the fight.

Turn to page 13.

Your mother Thetis is very pleased with your decision and smiles contentedly as she departs. You, however, feel a certain emptiness inside. While you look forward to your life of simple pleasures, you feel that something is missing. You look around your humble home and, while pleased, feel some dissatisfaction with the plainness of it all.

You realize suddenly that you, however long or short your life may be, belong on the battlefield. But is it too late? You sprint outside to stop your comrades before they leave. But your heart sinks as you see the sails of the Greek ships fading into the horizon. You turn back to your home forlorn, understanding that this life, without any glory or fame, is yours forever, and you will be forever dissatisfied with it.

THE END

"Athena and your mother Thetis wait while Hephaestus' Cyclopes
make the armor you need to avenge Patroclus' death."

You know that she is correct. You know that you must wait for armor if you are to have any chance of avenging Patroclus' death. You swallow your rage, but reserve it for when you will meet his killer on the battlefield.

The wait is interminable. But Thetis eventually returns with new armor created by Hephaestus himself, the god of blacksmiths. You receive it with pride and assemble the Greeks. You regret what has happened, you say, but are ready now to fight the Trojans, and bring victory to the Greeks. Agamemnon thanks you and reiterates that the gifts he offered you before are still yours. You decline; all you want is Trojan blood.

Turn to page 24.

Your mother Thetis smiles proudly. She loves you more than anything and is willing to see your comrades killed if it will mean an increase in your glory. She promises to speak to Zeus the thunderer.

The Trojans and Greeks have agreed to a cease-fire. But Zeus inspires the Trojans to break the cease-fire, and the Trojans gain the upper hand.

The battle rages for days, seesawing back and forth, but eventually the Trojans advance on the Greeks. They have left their walls and set up camp in the plain outside Troy so that they can attack the Greek ships the next morning and trap the Greeks on the beach.

The Greek leaders are worried. Agamemnon is regretting what he did to you; he can certainly use your help.

Turn to page 25.

Your anger is too great. You cannot allow Agamemnon to insult you so blatantly before your men. Immediately, your warrior instinct kicks in. Your sword is drawn. It is raised above the head of Agamemnon, prepared to avenge your honor in the only way you know how.

Suddenly, however, you feel your arms tighten. Your sword grows heavy, and your resolve is not so strong. Strangely, you feel a tugging on the long hair that flows out the back of your helmet and marks you as an adult Greek male.

You turn to see a vision of the goddess Athena. She warns you not to avenge yourself on Agamemnon in this way but to wait for a better opportunity. You have a choice to make.

If you choose to listen to Athena and spare Agamemnon, turn to page 38.

If you choose to ignore Athena and kill Agamemnon, turn to page 29.

23

You rush out to battle. The gods are with you. Trojans fall before you in countless number. But no matter. You want Patroclus' killer, the great Trojan warrior Hector, and will not stop until you have him.

Finally, you see Hector across the battlefield. You move toward him, but he sees you and runs. Finally, he can run no further and turns to face you. But before you fight, he addresses you: "Mighty Achilles, one of us will die here today. That we cannot deny. Let us make a pact, however, that, although we are mortal enemies, we will treat each other's body with the respect that the dead deserve. May we preserve our honor in this hateful time of war."

If you agree to Hector's suggestion, turn to page 5.

If you refuse Hector's suggestion, turn to page 35.

You see approaching your tent a group of three Greeks, a group of three friends: Odysseus, Phoenix, and Ajax. You greet them warmly; it has been a while since you've seen them. You invite them to stay, and you all have dinner together. After dinner, they present their proposal.

Agamemnon needs your help to defeat the Trojans. They are advancing on the Greeks, and the Greeks have lost the will and momentum to stop them. If you return, you will receive riches and plunder and the girl Briseis, whom Agamemnon wrongly took from you. Agamemnon regrets how he insulted you and wants to make amends.

You have a choice to make.

If you decide to accept Agamemnon's apology and return to battle, turn to page 18.

If you decide to refuse Agamemnon's apology and remain in your camp, turn to page 33.

The wind in your hair makes you feel alive. It reminds you why you're here and what you're doing. You have one goal now, and one goal only: find Patroclus' killer, the great Trojan warrior Hector, and avenge Patroclus' death.

The battlefield lies before you. Bodies are strewn about. You don't even notice. You don't hear the cheers as the Greeks see you approach. You don't hear the cries as the Trojans realize it's you. And you don't feel the fear that everyone else does when they realize that you are striding into battle without any armor.

The first Trojans you find are in fact so shocked that you dispense them easily. But it only gives you a false sense of confidence. Soon you are surrounded by Trojans. Your sword slashes the air and the Trojans, and they fall easily. But they are immediately replaced. You feel their swords piercing your side, your chest, your arms, your legs. You weaken but do not fall. But finally you feel it. Your only vulnerable spot. Your heel. And you feel the pain that you know signals the end. Your impending death, however, is hardly as shameful as your inability to avenge your friend's death.

THE END

Your advisors calm you and your understandable urgency for revenge. You agree to postpone the revolt until more men can be persuaded to join you.

In the meantime, you continue fighting as if nothing is wrong. In fact, you fight even harder than ever, and the Greeks reaffirm your status as the greatest of their warriors.

You urge the Greeks to continue fighting, to press on after the Trojans. The battle will be yours today, and then you can remove Agamemnon as Greek leader with the city of Troy in your hands!

Continue to the next page.

But as the day wears on, the Greek army grows thinner and thinner. You continue to tear through the Trojans, but your comrades fall beside you. Eventually, you realize that you alone have withstood the Trojans that day. But you cannot take the city by yourself.

As the fallen Greeks are brought back to camp, you see many of your friends and allies now dead. You hang your head in mourning for your lost comrades.

But in your grief, you fail to realize that many of the dead are those very men who were to aid you in your revolt against Agamemnon. You soon realize that, because of your hesitation and rage in battle, any chance of replacing Agamemnon as Greek leader has vanished.

You realize sadly that your honor will never be fully restored. You fight on, but only as half the warrior you once were. The Greeks may win this war, but without you as their hero.

THE END

Athena's attempts, however valiant and well intentioned, are too late. Vigor and strength return to your limbs, and you bring a crushing blow down on the head of Agamemnon. Every fiber of your warrior self screams with righteousness and revenge, and you glory in the death of the man who insulted your honor.

The Greeks, however, do not seem as awed by your strength. They look at you now, not with the respect and admiration they used to, but with a mixture of fear and disgust. Involuntarily you shrink before them, suddenly aware of what you have done and what it means.

Your glory as the premier Greek warrior has passed. You have crossed a line that cannot be recrossed. You now only await their decision: banishment or death. Either way, for you this war is over.

THE END

Your mother Thetis smiles proudly as she departs. She has heard your prayer and travels to the battlefield. A cease-fire has been called, but Thetis in a dream comes to Agamemnon and encourages him to attack: the Trojans are vulnerable, and victory is within reach.

Agamemnon musters the Greeks and formulates a plan. The army takes the Trojans by surprise and immediately gains an advantage. Quickly messengers are sent to your tent: the Greeks are winning, and Agamemnon wants you to join the fight to partake of the glory.

If you accept the invitation to join the fight,
turn to page 10.

If you continue to nurse your injured honor,
turn to page 2.

Quietly, you begin to recruit to your cause comrades who are similarly disappointed with Agamemnon. There are not as many as you originally thought, but enough to mount a successful revolt.

Those that you have chosen as your advisors urge you to bide your time and wait for a more opportune moment. Why fight with fewer men when time may yield you more?

You, however, feel that your group must strike while the insult is still fresh in the minds of the soldiers; their support is essential for the success of your mission.

If you choose to listen to your advisors and postpone the revolt, turn to page 27.

If you choose to follow your instinct and begin the revolt immediately, turn to page 55.

You see the look of fear in Hector's eyes and move toward him quickly. You know now that victory is yours, and you kill Hector easily with one thrust of your spear. The Trojan hero is dead.

You pause for a moment and soak in the cheers of your Greek compatriots as they crowd around you. Their shouts call for further violence. You feel their anger toward the Trojan champion and you feel satisfaction for avenging Patroclus' death. You have a choice to make.

If you listen to your compatriots and further defile Hector's dead body, turn to page 57.

If you ignore your companions and care for Hector's body, turn to page 12.

As happy as you are to see your friends, their entreaties amuse you. To think that you would put aside your anger and shame so easily at the mere mention of gifts and riches! Even the return of Briseis, the girl whose removal began this chain of events, isn't enough to soften you.

You calmly and politely decline the offer. You refute their arguments one by one. You send them away unhappy. They return to the Greek army and report your decision. The army is disheartened, but agrees that they have no other choice but to fight on without you.

You remain in your camp, firm in your resolve. You pray for your comrades' safety, but cannot put aside your resentment of Agamemnon. You wonder if you will ever fight in this war again.

Turn to page 49.

You want to help your friend, but the physical and emotional strain of the day is too much for you. Even as you begin to plan the funeral in your mind, you feel your eyes growing heavy. You sink back into your bed, unable to fight the rush of sleep that your body cannot resist. As you drift off into a deep, deep sleep, the last image before you is your friend Patroclus, with his head hung low. Worse than his disappointment in you is your knowledge that you selfishly betrayed your best friend and his wishes. You will have to live with this shame for the rest of your life. You will wake up tomorrow and even bury Patroclus, but you can never recover from your failure of him.

THE END

Hector's suggestion makes you laugh: "I have neither love nor respect for you, enemy Trojan. I will kill you and do whatever I want with your body. My friend Patroclus, whom you killed, will be avenged. The talking is finished. Prepare yourself."

The fight begins furiously. You cast your spear at Hector, and it misses. But the goddess Athena is with you; she returns your spear to you, and you ready yourself for Hector's attack. Hector's spear misses. Hector calls to his brother, who is acting as his squire, for another spear. But Hector is deceived. Athena has taken the form of Hector's brother and now assures your victory; he receives no other spear. Hector realizes the deception, understands what it means, and sees his death approaching.

Turn to page 32.

"You sit quietly as you contemplate lending Patroclus your armor."

Patroclus continues: "If you will not fight, at least let the Greeks think you are fighting. Give me your armor to wear. I will charge into battle in your armor and rouse the Greek troops. If they cannot look to you for inspiration, at least let them look to your armor. In your armor, with your armor before the troops, I can lead the Greeks against the Trojans; we can turn the Trojans back from the ships and avoid defeat."

You sit quietly for a moment as Patroclus' suggestion sinks in. You deliberate for a moment as you weigh the options. Finally, you speak:

If you agree to allow Patroclus to wear your armor into battle, turn to page 11.

If you refuse to allow Patroclus to wear your armor into battle, turn to page 41.

"Achilles, you must trust me. You will be avenged against Agamemnon, but killing him will not serve your purpose." You know she's right. And, however difficult, you swallow your anger and your pride and return your sword to its scabbard. Agamemnon will live. For now.

But another problem remains: your insulted honor. Although you have agreed not to kill Agamemnon, that doesn't prevent you from trying to regain your honor. But how much is your honor worth to you? What are you willing to do to regain it? How much shame are you willing to endure for your comrades?

You have three choices.

Continue to the next page to assess your choices.

1. You came to Troy to do a job and to honor a vow. You swore to defend Helen and her husband if anything happens, and you, of all the Greeks, are the man who can accomplish that most effectively. You can continue to fight, despite your injured honor.

2. You came to Troy to do a job and to honor a vow. But your honor is your honor and without that it is impossible to do your job effectively. You can remove yourself from the battle until you feel your honor has been restored sufficiently; the Greeks can see what it's like to fight without their best warrior.

3. You came to Troy to do a job and to honor a vow. But how can you do your job with such poor leadership? You can gather allies among your troops and remove Agamemnon as leader. You then can lead the Greeks to victory, as you were meant to.

If you continue to fight, turn to page 16.

If you remove yourself from battle, turn to page 43.

If you revolt against Agamemnon, turn to page 31.

Messengers keep you informed about the course of the battle. You nod knowingly as the news comes in; of course you were correct. The Greeks, thinking you were in the lead, inspired by the sight of your armor (if not you yourself), easily were able to push the Trojans back from the ships and put out the fire that they had set.

Success. Patroclus should be returning soon. His job done, the Trojans pushed back from the ships, he will leave the rest of the day to the Greeks, as you told him to.

But the day wears on, and Patroclus does not return. Your messengers tell you that he has felled Sarpedon, one of the Trojans' best warriors. They cheer for him and praise his strength. But you are afraid. Sarpedon is a mighty warrior. Patroclus may have escaped his sword, but how many other swords will now be pointed at him?

You see more messengers coming. This time their heads are bowed.

Turn to page 47.

"Patroclus, know that I love you like a brother. If anyone could wear my armor into battle, it is you. But my anger toward Agamemnon and the Greeks is greater than any love I feel for you. It may pain you to hear it, but it is true. I cannot agree to your request. The war will run its course without any involvement from me or my armor. I am sorry, but I cannot assent." Patroclus' face falls. But he understands and retreats to his tent.

The smell of burning wood is your first clue that the Greeks are defeated. You see the smoke rising above the ships, growing blacker and blacker as more ships catch fire. Soon the Trojans will be coming for you. For a moment, you imagine the confrontation. You only wonder whether it will be preferable to be killed or to be captured. Either way, you realize that, in terms of the war, for you this is . . .

THE END

You awaken the next day refreshed and eager for the battle. But as your squire dresses you for battle, you feel a gnawing inside: something doesn't feel right. You push it aside, chalking it up to pre-battle nerves. Dressed in all your splendor, you emerge to lead your men into battle.

As you survey your men before you, you recognize that something has changed. It is unspoken. It is subtle. But you can see in their eyes that they are looking at you differently.

Continue to page 17.

Your anger consumes you. Blind with rage and yearning so desperately to exact revenge on Agamemnon, you nonetheless restrain yourself and retreat to your camp. You communicate through your lieutenants that, until your honor is restored, you will remain removed from the battle; the Greeks can fight without you.

Finally alone, however, your anger does not subside. Still seething, you pray to your mother Thetis to help you. She alone can accomplish what must be accomplished.

If you pray to Thetis to come to the assistance of your comrades and help them to defeat the Trojans in your absence, turn to page 30.

If you pray to Thetis to come to the aid of your enemy, the Trojans, so that the Greeks might experience defeat without you, turn to page 22.

The appearance of Patroclus' ghost awakens you immediately. You spring from bed just as dawn's rosy fingers stretch across the land around you. You assemble the Greeks quickly for this grim duty. With everyone present, you salute Patroclus and light his funeral pyre. He will indeed find rest in the afterlife quickly; that is the least you can do for your best friend.

After the funeral, you declare a period of commemoration. You will host a series of athletic contests to honor Patroclus. The games continue through the day until finally the Greeks return to their tents exhausted. You too return to your tent to enjoy a meal with two of your captains. As you eat, you hear a scuffle outside your tent. An old man enters and raises his eyes to yours.

It is Priam, the king of Troy and the father of Hector, Patroclus' killer.

Continue to the next page.

Instinctively you reach for your sword upon seeing your enemy. But something about his face stops you. Before you can figure out what it is, he speaks: "Achilles, son of Peleus, I come asking for your pity and your compassion. You are indeed the greatest of Greek warriors; you killed our champion, my son, Hector. I ask now only that you return his body to me so that I may bury him properly. Let me do for him what you did for Patroclus."

At the mention of your best friend's name, you boil with anger, but check yourself before this unprecedented request. You have a choice to make.

If you choose to honor Priam's request and return Hector's body to him, turn to page 53.

If you choose to refuse Priam's request and keep Hector's body, turn to page 50.

"Patroclus is dead. Your wail of grief is so loud
that it is heard even by the gods."

You spring up to meet the messengers. Their eyes tell you what words don't need to. They say it anyway. Patroclus is dead.

Your wail of grief is so loud that it is heard even by the gods. Your mother Thetis appears, and you two mourn as one. Both of you know that you must now reenter the battle to avenge your friend's death, and that you will never return to Greece.

You spring up and call for your armor, forgetting of course that it is with Patroclus on the battlefield. You only hope that it is still with the body, but you know what you would do if the situation were reversed. That armor, especially belonging to the great Achilles, is now the trophy for some Trojan to wear in triumph.

No matter. Your anger is such that you are prepared to rush in without armor. Your mother stops you, though: "Wait, my son. I will get you new armor. Do not be hasty."

If you decide to listen to your mother and wait, turn to page 21.

If you decide to ignore your mother's advice, turn to page 26.

You have been fighting with little enthusiasm for almost a month now. The Greeks continue to press the Trojans back under your leadership. After a long day of battle, you return to the Greek camp. As you return to your tent, you overhear Agamemnon.

"The Trojans are within our reach. Under my leadership, we will overrun them, and then you will all proclaim me the greatest Greek warrior ever to live."

Your ears burn with rage as you hear Agamemnon steal your credit and your reputation. You may have been able to overlook your insulted honor the first time, but this you cannot stomach.

You continue toward your tent, but this time you will not return. You leave the next morning from Troy without a word of departure to anyone. Certainly not to Agamemnon.

THE END

The battle continues to rage. The Trojans continue to press toward the Greek ships. The Greek army is weakening. The Greek army is losing heart. You pity the Greeks. But you also know that you cannot help them.

Your best friend Patroclus approaches. You love and trust Patroclus like a brother. If there is anyone in this war that can convince you, it is he. But because he is such a good friend, he knows better than to try to convince you. He has another plan.

"Achilles," he begins. "The Greeks need you. They will be defeated without you. But I know why you remain out of the war and I understand, even if I don't agree. I can't, however, stand by while our comrades die around us. We must emerge from this war victorious. Greece depends on us. I would never ask you to enter the war when you choose not to. I do, however, ask you this."

Turn to page 37.

You have no pity for your enemy's father. You laugh out loud at his pathetic request. "Why should I not kill you now, Trojan king? That way we can all go home and be done with this war. Because of your courage to come here, I will let you leave with your life; because of your stupidity for coming here, I will let you leave without your son. Him I will keep as my trophy of the war and as a message to any who would cross me."

Priam realizes that he cannot change your mind and leaves with his head low. You wonder if you see his shoulders heave as he sobs. You think of your father. What if the roles were reversed? What if it were your body lying there in the hands of the enemy? You immediately move to recall Priam and return to him his son. But it is too late. He is gone and you are left with an emptiness you know will never be filled. Tomorrow, you will return Hector's body and leave for home, disgraced. You may have succeeded as a warrior, but you have failed as a man.

THE END

You return to the Greek camp with Hector's body still dragging behind you. Time has not decreased your wrath toward him.

But Patroclus is still dead, and his body deserves respect. You know that he cannot enter the underworld until his body has been cremated and his ashes have been properly disposed of.

You and the Greeks spend the rest of the day preparing for Patroclus' funeral. The funeral pyre, the wooden structure upon which his body will be cremated, grows higher and higher. But the sun sinks lower and lower in the sky, and it is growing late. With the preparations completed, you and the Greeks head to your tents for a good night's sleep before the funeral tomorrow.

But in the middle of the night, you are awakened. It is Patroclus' ghost.

Continue to the next page.

"Asleep, Achilles? How could you have forgotten me? It was not until I died that you neglected me. Bury me so that I might pass through the Gate of Hades. I wait for my funeral so that I might find peace in death. And you sleep."

You rejoice to see your friend, even his ghost, and you move to embrace him. But as you throw your arms around him, they only grab the air as he disappears, and you are left alone in your tent, his words hanging in the air. You have a choice to make.

If you choose to listen to your friend's pleas and hurry to bury him, turn to page 44.

If you choose to ignore your friend's pleas and go back to sleep, turn to page 34.

You consider carefully Priam's request. If he has made it through the Greek camp to your tent, he must be blessed by the gods; no enemy, even the most skilled warrior, much less an old man, could make it to your tent unharmed without the help of the gods.

And you think of your father. What if the roles were reversed? What if it were your body lying there in the hands of the enemy? Your heart breaks with pity for the old king, and you embrace him as you would your own father.

You explain that Hector's body has been well cared for; the gods must have been watching over it. But you send two servants to complete any final preparations for its return. You then invite Priam to join you at your table as your honored guest.

Continue to the next page.

Priam smiles briefly before he speaks: "Achilles, you have been more than kind and compassionate in your dealing with me. But let us not forget that we are still at war. Perhaps at another time, in different circumstances, we can sit at table together and share a meal. But right now, I am still a Trojan in the Greek camp. I will not tempt fate any more than I have already." He pauses. "Thank you."

You allow yourself a smile as you watch Priam leave with his son's body. You know you have made the right decision. You boiled with anger toward Hector when he killed your best friend, but your anger has subsided. He belongs with his father now. That is his fate.

Turn to page 59.

Despite your advisors' pleas, you know that success comes to those who do not hesitate. You formulate a plan, present it to your advisors, and prepare to attack on the morning of the day after next.

The next day passes interminably as you eagerly await the moment of revolt. It is not in your nature to be patient, even for the short span of a day. Eventually, however, night falls, and you sleep, confident that the next time you lie down, you will be the leader of the Greek army.

Turn to page 58.

"As you drag Hector's body, you feel twisted satisfaction
in the cries of horror you hear."

Your anger over Patroclus' death cannot subside. You hear your companions cheering over Hector's dead body, and your wrath consumes you. You are not finished with him yet.

You look to the walls of Troy as you tie Hector's dead body to your chariot. As you drag Hector's body around the walls of Troy three times for all of his people to see, something somewhere feels wrong, but you are too angry to wonder why. You can only think of your friend Patroclus and what this Trojan did to him. You feel twisted satisfaction in the cries of horror that you can hear coming from the Trojan walls as Hector's body passes.

Turn to page 51.

Dawn comes, and you prepare for battle, this time in your own camp. You do not like the idea of dissent within an army, but Agamemnon can no longer lead the army effectively.

Revolt is your only option, you think as you prepare to step outside, meet your men, and take Agamemnon by surprise.

But as you part the flap of your tent, a surprise awaits. Agamemnon himself stands before you, a troop of men behind him with their swords drawn. Only a momentary flicker of surprise passes over your face; you realize crushingly that one of your advisors must have lost heart and informed Agamemnon of your plan.

You know, even as the greatest warrior among the Greeks, you could not withstand a force of your own comrades of this size. You bow your head in a sign of submission. If you are lucky, you will be sent home in disgrace. If not . . .

THE END

And you realize that, despite the inhumanity that surrounds you in this hateful war and your own sometimes selfish behavior, in the end you have regained even a small part of yourself that recalls the compassion and humanity that you left at home when you came to Troy. Indeed, Achilles . . .

Continue to the next page.

YOU HAVE SUCCESSFULLY
FOLLOWED YOUR FATE!

GLOSSARY OF NAMES

Achilles *[ah – KILL – eez]*. Greatest of the Greek warriors who fought at Troy.

Agamemnon *[agg – ah – MEM – non]*. Greek general who, with his brother MENELAUS led the Greek army against Troy to recover HELEN, the wife of MENELAUS whom PARIS kidnapped.

Ajax *[AY – jacks]*. Great Greek warrior sent as part of an embassy to petition ACHILLES to return to battle by AGAMEMNON.

Athena *[ah – THEE – nah]*. Goddess of wisdom, loyal to the Greek army.

Briseis *[brih – SEE – iss]*. Trojan priest's daughter whom ACHILLES won in battle and whom AGAMEMNON claimed as his own.

Hector *[HECK – tor]*. Greatest of the Trojan warriors, killed by the great Greek warrior ACHILLES.

Helen *[HELL – in]*. Wife of the Greek general MENELAUS. She was kidnapped by PARIS, which was the cause of the Trojan War.

Hephaestus *[heh – FES – tus]*. Blacksmith god who crafted new armor for ACHILLES.

Menelaus *[men – eh – LAY – us]*. Husband of HEL-EN who, with his brother AGAMEMNON, led the Greek forces to Troy to recover HELEN after she was kidnapped by PARIS.

Patroclus *[pah – TROK – lus]*. Loyal companion of ACHILLES who is killed by HECTOR in the Trojan War.

Peleus *[PEE – lee – us]*. Mortal father of ACHILLES and husband of THETIS.

Phoenix *[FEE – nicks]*. Older Greek soldier sent as part of an embassy to petition ACHILLES to return to battle by AGAMEMNON.

Priam *[PRY – am]*. King of Troy and father of HECTOR.

Sarpedon *[sar – PEE – don]*. Mighty Trojan warrior killed in battle by PATROCLUS.

Thetis *[THEE – tiss]*. Minor sea goddess and mother of ACHILLES.

Zeus *[ZOOS]*. King of the gods and god of thunder.

This Book
Belongs To:

_____

LIBRARY *of* CLASSIC POETS

Robert Frost

Selected Poems

Elizabeth Barrett Browning: Selected Poems

Emily Dickinson: Selected Poems

Robert Frost: Selected Poems

Henry Wadsworth Longfellow: Selected Poems

Edgar Allan Poe: Complete Poems

Carl Sandburg: Selected Poems

Walt Whitman: Selected Poems

William Butler Yeats: Selected Poems

Robert Frost

Selected Poems

Gramercy Books
New York

This 2004 edition is published by Gramercy Books, an imprint of Random
House Value Publishing, a division of Random House, Inc., New York.

Gramercy is a registered trademark and the colophon
is a trademark of Random House, Inc.

Random House
New York • Toronto • London • Sydney • Auckland
www.randomhouse.com

Printed and bound in the United States of America

This work was originally published by Random House Value Publishing
in March 2001 in another format.

ISBN: 0-517-21508-X

Special Edition
9 8 7 6 5 4 3 2 1

CONTENTS

A Boy's Will

North of Boston

Mountain Interval

INTRODUCTION

Robert Lee Frost, whose poetry is so closely associated with the woods and streams and farms of New England, was born in San Francisco, California, on March 26, 1874; he was named after the famous Confederate general. When Robert Frost was eleven, his father died of tuberculosis. He moved with his mother and sister to Lawrence, Massachusetts, his father's hometown, and shortly thereafter to Salem, New Hampshire.

It was quite a change from the dangerous and exciting city on the Pacific, but in those boyhood years Frost devoted much time to baseball and rambles in the countryside with friends. In high school he became a serious student and editor of the school newspaper. He was elected class poet and was graduated valedictorian.

One of his early poems, "God's Garden," shows the influence of his deeply religious mother. In others, "Greece," "A Dream of Julius Caesar," and "Caesar's Lost Transport Ships," he expresses his interest in history and his idealization of heroic figures of the past. "La Noche Triste," a poem about the bravery of the Aztecs against the invasion of Cortes, was Frost's first published poem; it appeared in his school newspaper in 1892.

It was that year that Frost entered Dartmouth College, but he stayed less than one semester. His high school sweetheart and covaledictorian, Elinor White, continued studying at Saint Lawrence University, and this created problems between them: Frost wanted her to leave and marry him. During a particularly troubled period in 1894, to prove his love and devotion he had five poems that he had written to her privately printed. Two copies of *Twilight* were printed and bound, and contained the poems "Twilight," "Summering," "The Falls," "An Unhistoric Spot," and "My Butterfly," which had recently been published in *The Independent*, a nationally circulated periodical. His plan ended disastrously when he surprised Elinor at her school dormitory and was turned away. As he left the school he destroyed one of the copies of *Twilight*.

Eventually, Frost did marry Elinor White. In 1912, after several setbacks and disappointments (including a few years as chicken farmers), the Frosts moved to England with their four children. It was there that his first book of poems, *A Boy's Will*, was published. The title is taken from "My Lost Youth," a poem by Henry Wadsworth Longfellow: "A boy's will is the wind's will / And the thoughts of youth are long, long thoughts." The early poems in the book reflect the reckless, defiant attitudes of youth, while the later ones show a maturing poet who realizes his place in society.

"Into My Own," the first poem in *A Boy's Will*, in which the poet is sure that an escape from the world into "those dark trees" is desirable, provides an interesting contrast with "Stopping by Woods on a Snowy Evening," written several years later. Here although the dark woods are more inviting than ever, the poet knows that he has commitments and obligations to the world and to those he loves.

Several of the poems sprang from Frost's own experiences on his farm in Derry, New Hampshire. "Storm Fear," for example, is about the frightening, trapped feeling of being snowed in. The elation and hope that come with spring are evident in "To the Thawing Wind," which reads like an incantation.

The theme of finding in Nature the source of life, the source of the universe—a theme echoed in such later masterpieces as "West-Running Brook"—appears in the poem "In a Vale." A fanciful lyric about fairies, it reveals that Nature can teach much to those who know how to listen and observe.

In 1914, Frost's second book of poems, *North of Boston,* was also published in England. Critically well received, as *A Boy's Will* had been, it contains many long poems—dramatic dialogues and narratives. Developing his theme of opposing forces—both in nature and ourselves—Frost writes about a farmer and his wife visited by an old former farm worker; a professor sharing a hotel room with a talkative, disturbing stranger; the tension between a husband and wife who cannot share their grief over their dead child; a farm wife who is tired of her constant work but knows she must continue it; a disabled man receiving a pittance from his employer's lawyer.

North of Boston opens with the beautiful, short lyric "The Pasture." Other well-known poems are "After Apple-Picking," a beautiful piece filled with marvelous images about a weary man's thoughts about his full and busy life, and "The Wood-Pile," in which an image of waste and decay confronts a wanderer in the woods.

In 1915 Frost moved back to New Hampshire with his family. The following year *Mountain Interval* was published. Twelve of the thirty poems in this collection were written, at least in part, before *A Boy's Will* was published. *Mountain Interval* solidified and enlarged Frost's achievement and contains some of his finest work, including "The Road Not Taken" and "Birches," which were to become two of his most popular poems.

Perhaps more than any other poet, Robert Frost captured the voice of New England. A four-time winner of the Pulitzer Prize for poetry, he created a new poetic language that has a deep and timeless resonance.

GAIL HARVEY

New York
1992

Early Poems

GREECE

They say, "Let there be no more war!"
    And straightway, at the word,
Along the Mediterranean shore,
    The call to arms is heard.

Greece could not let her glory fade!
    Although peace be in sight,
The race the Persian wars arrayed
    Must fight one more good fight.

Greece! Rise triumphant. Long ago
    It was you proved to men
A few may countless hosts o'erthrow:
    Now prove it once again!

GOD'S GARDEN

God made a beauteous garden
   With lovely flowers strown,
But one straight, narrow pathway
   That was not overgrown.
And to this beauteous garden
   He brought mankind to live,
And said: "To you, my children,
   These lovely flowers I give.
Prune ye my vines and fig trees,
   With care my flowrets tend,
But keep the pathway open
   Your home is at the end."

Then came another master,
   Who did not love mankind,
And planted on the pathway
   Gold flowers for them to find.
And mankind saw the bright flowers,
   That, glitt'ring in the sun,
Quite hid the thorns of av'rice
   That poison blood and bone;
And far off many wandered,
   And when life's night came on,
They still were seeking gold flowers,
   Lost, helpless and alone.

O, cease to heed the glamour
    That blinds your foolish eyes,
Look upward to the glitter
    Of stars in God's clear skies.
Their ways are pure and harmless
    And will not lead astray,

But aid your erring footsteps
    To keep the narrow way.
And when the sun shines brightly
    Tend flowers that God has given
And keep the pathway open
    That leads you on to heaven.

LA NOCHE TRISTE

Tenochtitlan

Changed is the scene: the peace
And regal splendor which
Once that city knew are gone,
And war now reigns upon
That throng, who but
A week ago were all
Intent on joy supreme.
Cries of the wounded break
The stillness of the night,
Or challenge of the guard.
The Spaniard many days
Besieged within the place,
Where kings did rule of old,
Now pressed by hunger by
The all-relentless foe,
Looks for some channel of
Escape. The night is dark;
Black clouds obscure the sky—
A dead calm lies o'er all.
The heart of one is firm,
His mind is constant still,
To all, his word is law.
Cortes his plan hath made,
The time hath come. Each one
His chosen place now takes,
There waits the signal, that
Will start the long retreat.

DOWN THE BROOK. AND BACK.

I leave the meadow for the brook,
    Speed, speed, my icy carriers,
  Away, away, the black ice lies,
And where I glide on either side
  The woody midnight's rise—
    Speed, speed, speed on ye tarriers,
The ice-fields fall—a distant boom—
On, on, from gloom to deeper gloom—
    Speed, speed, let darkness follow.
Alone, alone, the breezes moan
Gives steel to steel; I wheel and reel
    On rippled ice and hollow.
The ice once more is smooth, before
  I swerve from brook to river,
    And as I dash, the muskrat's plash
Comes from the hazy, fleeing shore,
  Where first the moonbeams quiver.

The moon is up, and I am weary.
Beyond, the lane-like brook lies dreary;
Hours fleet, I stumble on o'er crusted snow;
With reeds the ice is bearded as I go.
Afar I wend, and I am weary,—
The clouded moon is dim and bleary.

THE FLIGHT

Anon the cry comes down the line,
The portals wide are swung,
A long dark line moves out the gate,
And now the flight's begun.

Aye, cautiously it moves at first,
As ship steered o'er the reef,
Looking for danger all unseen,
But which may bring to grief.

Straight for the causeway now they make,
The bridge is borne before,
'Tis ta'en and placed across the flood,
And all go trooping o'er.

Yet e'er the other side is reached,
Wafted along the wind,
The rolling of the snakeskin drum
Comes floating from behind.

And scarcely has its rolling ceased,
Than out upon the lake,
Where all was silence just before,
A conch the calm doth break.

What terror to each heart it bears,
That sound of ill portent,
Each gunner to escape now looks,
On safety all are bent.

Forward they press in wild despair,
On to the next canal,
Held on all sides by foe and sea,
Like deer within corral.

Now surging this way, now in that,
The mass sways to and fro,
The infidel around it sweeps—
Slowly the night doth go.

A war cry soundeth through the night,
The 'tzin! the 'tzin! is there,
His plume nods wildly o'er the scene,
Oh, Spaniard, now beware!

With gaping jaws the cannon stands,
Points it among the horde;
The valiant Leon waits beside
Ready with match and sword.

The 'tzin quick springeth to his side,
His mace he hurls on high,
It crasheth through the Spanish steel,
And Leon prone doth lie.

Falling, he died beneath his gun,—
He died at duty's call,
And many falling on that night,
Dying, so died they all.

The faithful guarders at the bridge,
Have worked with might and main,
Nor can they move it from its place,
Swollen by damp of rain.

On through the darkness comes the cry,
The cry that all is lost;
Then e'en Cortes takes up the shout,
And o'er the host 'tis tossed.

Some place their safety in the stream,
But sink beneath the tide,
E'en others crossing on the dead,
Thus reach the other side.

Surrounded and alone he sits,
Upon his faithful steed;
Here Alvarado clears a space,
But none might share the deed—

For darkness of that murky night
Hides deeds of brightest fame,
Which in the ages yet to come,
Would light the hero's name.

His faithful charger now hath fall'n,
Pierced to the very heart.
Quick steps he back, his war cry shouts,
Then onward doth he dart.

Runs he, and leaping high in air,
Fixed does he seem a space,
One instant and the deed is done,
He standeth face to face—

With those who on the other side
Their safety now have found.
The thirst for vengeance satisfied,
The Aztec wheels around.

So, as the sun climbs up the sky,
And shoots his dawning rays,
The foe, as parted by his dart,
Each go their sep'rate ways.

Upon the ground the dead men lie,
Trampled midst gold and gore,
The Aztec toward his temple goes,
For now the fight is o'er.

Follow we not the Spaniard more,
Wending o'er hill and plain,
Suffice to say he reached the coast,
Lost Fortune to regain.

The flame shines brightest e'er goes out,
Thus with the Aztec throne,
On that dark night before the end,
So o'er the fight it shone.

The Montezumas are no more,
Gone is their regal throne,
And freemen live, and rule, and die,
Where they have ruled alone.

SONG OF THE WAVE

"Rolling, rolling, o'er the deep,
Sunken treasures neath me sleep
As I shoreward slowly sweep.

Onward peacefully I roll,
Ever thoughtless of the goal,
Sea-bells round me chime and toll.

There is peace above, below,
Far beneath me sea-weeds grow,
Tiny fish glide to and fro,

Now in sunlight, now in shade,
Lost within some ocean glade
By the restless waters made.

Pushing onward as before,
Now descry the distant shore,
Hear the breakers sullen roar;

Quicken then my rolling pace,
With glad heart I join the race
O'er the white-capp'd glittering space,

Thinking naught of woe or grief,
Dancing, prancing, like a leaf,
Caring not for cliff or reef.

Lo! black cliffs above me loom,
Casting o'er me awful gloom,
And foretell my coming doom.

O! that I might reach the land,
Reach and lave the sunny sand,
But these rocks on every hand—

Seem my joyous course to stay,
Rise and bar my happy way,
Shutting out the sun's bright ray.

I must now my proud crest lower
And the wild sea roam no more."
Hark! the crash and mighty roar,
Then the wave's sport life is o'er.

A DREAM OF JULIUS CAESAR

A dreamy day; a gentle western breeze
That murmurs softly 'midst the sylvan shades;
Above, the fleecy clouds glide slowly on
To sink from view; within the forest's depth,
A thrush's drowsy note starts echoes through
The vistas of the overhanging trees.
All nature seems to weave a circle of
Enchantment round the mind, and give full sway
To flitting thoughts and dreams of bygone years.
Thus, as the summer afternoon wears on,
In Nature's cradle lulled to calm repose,
I watch the shifting of a purling rill,
As visions of a busy throng, of life,
Of passing days that come not back again,
Rush in confusion through my weary brain;
Till rumblings wafted o'er the distant hills,
Proclaim a timely warning to the one
Who, wandering far from shelter and from home,
Forgets that space exists, that still he lives:—
But, wrapped in Nature's all entrancing shroud,
Is lured to seek her wildest inmost realms.
The dying cadences are tossed from vale
To vale, but fall unheeded on my ear.
Anon, the winds burst on the silent scene,
And cause the leaves to dance and sing for joy.
Then clouds with bosoms darker than the night,
Rise up along the whole horizon's brink,
And all the sky is flecked with hurrying forms.
Thus, ever as the storm comes on, led by
The heralds of its wrathful power, between
The foremost rifts, like ladders long, by which
From earth to heaven the woodland nymphs may pass

Beyond the clouds, bright rays of light stretch down
Upon each grove and mead.

                            So, far and wide
A charm of magic breathes its spell around:
For at my feet a far upreaching ladder rests,
And as I gaze, a form, scarce seen at first,
Glides down; a moment, and before me stands,
With stately mien and noble wreathéd brow,
His toga streaming to the western wind,
The restless fire still gleaming in those eyes,
Just as before the Roman Senate, years
Agone, he stood and ruled a people with
His mighty will, Caesar, first conqueror of
The Roman World. Within his hand the bolt
Of Jove gleams forth with frequent flash. Clasping
The toga's waving folds, a gem of ray
Most pure, that nigh outshines the sun, rests like
The dew of heaven. I gaze in awe, a space;
Then, with majestic mien, he points me toward
A bridge, an ancient moss-grown trunk that fell
In some fierce storm to join the brook's green banks,
And speaks: "Be gone! from Jupiter I come
To rule with storm and darkness o'er the world,"
Then with uplifted arm: "Look up, behold
My might, my legions. Conquest still is the
One passion of this fiery breast. Speak thy
Farewell to all this scene of quietude
And peace; ere from this hand I launch the fire
Of Jove, and pierce the darkness with its gleam;
Ere yonder cohorts with resistless march
Spread terror in the air and vanquish light."
He speaks and vanishes from sight. The roar
Of chariot wheels breaks on my ear. The fight
Is on, for blood in torrents falls around,
Not crimson, but a lighter hue, such as
The fairy hosts of silvery light might shed.

CAESAR'S LOST TRANSPORT SHIPS

Some fell away to westward with the wind,
And one full darkly figured on the sun
At sunset; but the fight on Briton's beach
Got us a shelter under Dover Cliff,
And all night long a voice made wild lament
Circling the confines of the restless camp;
So that we had sad thoughts of those at sea.
There would no messenger come back from them!
Each one alone went leaping down the world
With no sail set, deserted on the deck,
And in the hull a tremor of low speech.
And overhead the petrel wafted wide.

PARTING. TO——

I dreamed the setting sun would rise no more.
My spirit fled; nor sought an aimless sun
Whirled madly on through pathless space, and free
Amid a world of worlds enthralled. Ah no!
But deep within a silent solitude
It lingered on. The twilight waned; across
The hills and dark'ning sky the west wind stole,
And broad-cast spread the sun-path gathered gold,
Undying memories of the hopeless dead.
The dew of sadness fell, and far into
The coming night of storm and calm I gazed.
Oh, sadness, who may tell what joy is thine?
A whisper breathed: "What lies unvoiced on earth
Is heaven sung." And gloom crept softly down
With longing deep as everlasting night.

THE TRAITOR

Seabird of the battle surf,
    Lorna is dead.
Black on Colla's castled hill
    Ruin is spread.
Weep for Lorna who rode forth
With his king against the North.

Lorna came again at morn,
    Riding from war.
Messenger of battle won,
    Tidings he bore:—
"Quenchless was the charge he made,
Low the insurgent walls were laid."

And while revelry was rife
    Through Colla's halls,
Then the lonely warder saw,
    Pacing the walls,
Eastward in the morning's grays,
Serried spears in the sunrise blaze.

By an altar in a vault—
    Night dripping dew—
Lorna's muffled cry arose;
    Bat-like it flew:—
"Sacrifice for victory!
Priest and victim find in me!"

Seabird of the battle surf,
    Lorna is dead.
Black on Colla's castled hill
    Ruin is spread.
Royal seal upon the tomb
Where he sleeps in endless gloom.

CLASS HYMN

There is a nook among the alders
Still sleeping to the catbird's "Hush";
   Below, a long stonebridge is bending
Above a runnel's silent rush.

   A dreamer hither often wanders
And gathers many a snow-white stone;
   He weighs them, poised upon his fingers,
Divining each one's silvery tone.

   He drops them! When the stream makes music,
Fair visions with its vault-voice swell:
   And so, for us, the future rises,
As thought-stones stir our heart's "Farewell!"

TWILIGHT

Why am I first in thy so sad regard,
O twilight gazing from I know not where?
I fear myself as one more than I guessed!
Am I instead of one so very fair?—
That thou art sorrowful and I oppressed?

High in the isolating air,
Over the inattentive moon,
Two birds sail on great wings,
    And vanish soon.
(And they leave the north sky bare!)

The far-felt solitudes that harbor night,
Wake to the singing of the wood-bird's fright.
By invocation, O wide silentness,
Thy spirit and my spirit pass in air!
They are unmemoried consciousness,
    Nor great nor less!
And thou art here and I am everywhere!

SUMMERING

I would arise and in a dream go on—
Not very far, not very far—and then
Lie down amid the sunny grass again,
And fall asleep till night-time or next dawn.

In sleepy self-sufficiency I'd turn;
I'd seek new comfort and be hard to please—
Far in a meadow by an isle of trees,
All summer long amid the grass and fern.

Forests would have to be all round about,
And the mead silent, and the grasses deep,
Else I might not gain such a tireless sleep!
I could not slumber if the wains were out!

THE FALLS

'Tis a steep wood of rocks,
With the fern grown everywhere;
But with no birds—not a wing!
And the falls come down there.
Even an Indian trail
Would swerve to a haunt so fair!
One used to—there were the ferns
And the falls came down there.

AN UNHISTORIC SPOT

Ah passionate is rest when to the earth
I yield in full length contact of sweet pain!
Here just within the bars in the chill grass,
And the great shadow of a fruitless tree,
I at once sleep and am awake in joy.
And when I sit half-conscious on the slope,
And lean upon one grass-wrought hand and gaze,
The lone thrush gurgles nectar in his throat,
On some green spire, adjusting his furled wings,
The local cricket quavers to the wind,
And every one that passes look at me.

THE BIRDS DO THUS

I slept all day,
　The birds do thus
That sing a while
　At eve for us.

To have you soon
　I gave away—
Well satisfied
　To give—a day.

Life's not so short
　I care to keep
The unhappy days;
　I choose to sleep.

WARNING

The day will come when you will cease to know,
　The heart will cease to tell you; sadder yet,
Tho you say o'er and o'er what once you knew,
　You will forget, you will forget.

There is no memory for what is true,
　The heart once silent. Well may you regret,
Cry out upon it, that you have known all
　But to forget, but to forget.

Blame no one but yourself for this, lost soul!
　I feared it would be so that day we met
Long since, and you were changed. And I said then,
　He will forget, he will forget.

QUEST OF THE ORCHIS

I felt the chill of the meadow underfoot,
  But the sun o'erhead;
And snatches of verse and song of scenes like this
  I sung or said.

I skirted the margin alders for miles and miles
  In a sweeping line;
The day was the day by every flower that blooms,
  But I saw no sign.

Yet further I went before the scythes should come,
  For the grass was high;
Till I saw the path where the slender fox had come
  And gone panting by.

Then at last and following that I found—
  In the very hour
When the color flushed to the petals, it must have
  been—
    The far-sought flower.

There stood the purple spires, with no breath of air
  Or headlong bee
To disturb their perfect poise the livelong day
  'Neath the aldertree!

I only knelt and, putting the boughs aside,
  Looked, or at most
Counted them all to the buds in the copse's depth,
  Pale as a ghost.

Then I arose and silent wandered home,
  And I for one
Said that the fall might come and whirl of leaves,
  For summer was done.

A Boy's Will

INTO MY OWN

One of my wishes is that those dark trees,
So old and firm they scarcely show the breeze,
Were not, as 'twere, the merest mask of gloom,
But stretched away unto the edge of doom.

I should not be withheld but that some day
Into their vastness I should steal away,
Fearless of ever finding open land,
Or highway where the slow wheel pours the
     sand.

I do not see why I should e'er turn back,
Or those should not set forth upon my track
To overtake me, who should miss me here
And long to know if still I held them dear.

They would not find me changed from him
     they knew—
Only more sure of all I thought was true.

GHOST HOUSE

I dwell in a lonely house I know
That vanished many a summer ago,
    And left no trace but the cellar walls,
    And a cellar in which the daylight falls,
And the purple-stemmed wild raspberries grow.

O'er ruined fences the grapevines shield
The woods come back to the mowing field;
    The orchard tree has grown one copse
    Of new wood and old where the woodpecker
       chops;
The footpath down to the well is healed.

I dwell with a strangely aching heart
In that vanished abode there far apart
    On that disused and forgotten road
    That has no dust bath now for the toad.
Night comes; the black bats tumble and dart;

The whippoorwill is coming to shout
And hush and cluck and flutter about:
    I hear him begin far enough away
    Full many a time to say his say
Before he arrives to say it out.

It is under the small, dim, summer star,
I know not who these mute folk are
    Who share the unlit place with me—
    Those stones out under the low-limbed tree
Doubtless bear names that the mosses mar.

They are tireless folk, but slow and sad,
Though two, close-keeping, are lass and lad,—
    With none among them that ever sings,
    And yet, in view of how many things,
As sweet companions as might be had.

MY NOVEMBER GUEST

My sorrow, when she's here with me,
   Thinks these dark days of autumn rain
Are beautiful as days can be;
She loves the bare, the withered tree;
   She walks the sodden pasture lane.

Her pleasure will not let me stay.
   She talks and I am fain to list:
She's glad the birds are gone away,
She's glad her simple worsted gray
   Is silver now with clinging mist.

The desolate, deserted trees,
   The faded earth, the heavy sky,
The beauties she so truly sees,
She thinks I have no eye for these,
   And vexes me for reason why.

Not yesterday I learned to know
   The love of bare November days
Before the coming of the snow,
But it were vain to tell her so,
   And they are better for her praise.

A LATE WALK

When I go up through the mowing field,
  The headless aftermath,
Smooth-laid like thatch with the heavy dew,
  Half closes the garden path.

And when I come to the garden ground,
  The whir of sober birds
Up from the tangle of withered weeds
  Is sadder than any words.

A tree beside the wall stands bare,
  But a leaf that lingered brown,
Disturbed, I doubt not, by my thought,
  Comes softly rattling down.

I end not far from my going forth
  By picking the faded blue
Of the last remaining aster flower
  To carry again to you.

LOVE AND A QUESTION

A stranger came to the door at eve,
    And he spoke the bridegroom fair.
He bore a green-white stick in his hand,
    And, for all burden, care.
He asked with the eyes more than the lips
    For a shelter for the night,
And he turned and looked at the road afar
    Without a window light.

The bridegroom came forth into the porch
    With "Let us look at the sky,
And question what of the night to be,
    Stranger, you and I."
The woodbine leaves littered the yard,
    The woodbine berries were blue,
Autumn, yes, winter was in the wind;
    "Stranger, I wish I knew."

Within, the bride in the dusk alone
    Bent over the open fire,
Her face rose-red with the glowing coal
    And the thought of the heart's desire.

The bridegroom looked at the weary road,
    Yet saw but her within,
And wished her heart in a case of gold
    And pinned with a silver pin.

The bridegroom thought it little to give
    A dole of bread, a purse,
A heartfelt prayer for the poor of God,
    Or for the rich a curse;

But whether or not a man was asked
    To mar the love of two
By harboring woe in the bridal house,
    The bridegroom wished he knew.

STARS

How countlessly they congregate
  O'er our tumultuous snow,
Which flows in shapes as tall as trees
  When wintry winds do blow!—

As if with keenness for our fate,
  Our faltering few steps on
To white rest, and a place of rest
  Invisible at dawn,—

And yet with neither love nor hate,
  Those stars like some snow-white
Minerva's snow-white marble eyes
  Without the gift of sight.

STORM FEAR

When the wind works against us in the dark,
And pelts with snow
The lower chamber window on the east,
And whispers with a sort of stifled bark,
The beast,
"Come out! Come out!"—
It costs no inward struggle not to go,
Ah, no!
I count our strength,
Two and a child,
Those of us not asleep subdued to mark
How the cold creeps as the fire dies at length,—
How drifts are piled,
Dooryard and road ungraded,
Till even the comforting barn grows far away
And my heart owns a doubt
Whether 'tis in us to arise with day
And save ourselves unaided.

WIND AND WINDOW FLOWER

Lovers, forget your love,
    And list to the love of these,
She a window flower,
    And he a winter breeze.

When the frosty window veil
    Was melted down at noon,
And the caged yellow bird
    Hung over her in tune,

He marked her through the pane,
    He could not help but mark,
And only passed her by,
    To come again at dark.

He was a winter wind,
    Concerned with ice and snow,
Dead weeds and unmated birds,
    And little of love could know.

But he sighed upon the sill,
    He gave the sash a shake,
As witness all within
    Who lay that night awake.

Perchance he half prevailed
    To win her for the flight
From the firelit looking glass
    And warm stove-window light.

But the flower leaned aside
    And thought of naught to say,
And morning found the breeze
    A hundred miles away.

TO THE THAWING WIND

Come with rain, O loud Southwester!
Bring the singer, bring the nester;
Give the buried flower a dream;
Make the settled snowbank steam;
Find the brown beneath the white;
But whate'er you do tonight,
Bathe my window, make it flow,
Melt it as the ices go;
Melt the glass and leave the sticks
Like a hermit's crucifix;
Burst into my narrow stall;
Swing the picture on the wall;
Run the rattling pages o'er;
Scatter poems on the floor;
Turn the poet out of door.

A PRAYER IN SPRING

Oh, give us pleasure in the flowers today;
And give us not to think so far away
As the uncertain harvest; keep us here
All simply in the springing of the year.

Oh, give us pleasure in the orchard white,
Like nothing else by day, like ghosts by night;
And make us happy in the happy bees,
The swarm dilating round the perfect trees.

And make us happy in the darting bird
That suddenly above the bees is heard,
The meteor that thrusts in with needle bill,
And off a blossom in midair stands still.

For this is love and nothing else is love,
The which it is reserved for God above
To sanctify to what far ends He will,
But which it only needs that we fulfil.

FLOWER-GATHERING

I left you in the morning,
And in the morning glow,
You walked a way beside me
To make me sad to go.
Do you know me in the gloaming,
Gaunt and dusty gray with roaming?
Are you dumb because you know me not,
Or dumb because you know?

All for me? And not a question
For the faded flowers gay
That could take me from beside you
For the ages of a day?
They are yours, and be the measure
Of their worth for you to treasure,
The measure of the little while
That I've been long away.

ROSE POGONIAS

A saturated meadow,
    Sun-shaped and jewel-small,
A circle scarcely wider
    Than the trees around were tall;
Where winds were quite excluded,
    And the air was stifling sweet
With the breath of many flowers,—
    A temple of the heat.

There we bowed us in the burning,
    As the sun's right worship is,
To pick where none could miss them
    A thousand orchises;
For though the grass was scattered,
    Yet every second spear
Seemed tipped with wings of color,
    That tinged the atmosphere.

We raised a simple prayer
    Before we left the spot,
That in the general mowing
    That place might be forgot;
Or if not all so favored,
    Obtain such grace of hours,
That none should mow the grass there
    While so confused with flowers.

ASKING FOR ROSES

A house that lacks, seemingly, mistress and master,
   With doors that none but the wind ever closes,
Its floor all littered with glass and with plaster;
   It stands in a garden of old-fashioned roses.

I pass by that way in the gloaming with Mary;
   "I wonder," I say, "who the owner of those is."
"Oh, no one you know," she answers me airy,
   "But one we must ask if we want any roses."

So we must join hands in the dew coming coldly
   There in the hush of the wood that reposes,
And turn and go up to the open door boldly,
   And knock to the echoes as beggars for roses.

"Pray, are you within there, Mistress Who-were-you?"
   'Tis Mary that speaks and our errand discloses.
"Pray, are you within there? Bestir you, bestir you!
   'Tis summer again; there's two come for roses.

"A word with you, that of the singer recalling—
   Old Herrick: a saying that every maid knows is
A flower unplucked is but left to the falling,
   And nothing is gained by not gathering roses."

We do not loosen our hands' intertwining
   (Not caring so very much what she supposes),
There when she comes on us mistily shining
   And grants us by silence the boon of her roses.

WAITING

Afield at Dusk

What things for dream there are when specter-like,
Moving among tall haycocks lightly piled,
I enter alone upon the stubble field,
From which the laborers' voices late have died,
And in the antiphony of afterglow
And rising full moon, sit me down
Upon the full moon's side of the first haycock
And lose myself amid so many alike.

I dream upon the opposing lights of the hour,
Preventing shadow until the moon prevail;
I dream upon the nighthawks peopling heaven,
Each circling each with vague unearthly cry,
Or plunging headlong with fierce twang afar;
And on the bat's mute antics, who would seem
Dimly to have made out my secret place,
Only to lose it when he pirouettes,
And seek it endlessly with purblind haste;

On the last swallow's sweep; and on the rasp
In the abyss of odor and rustle at my back,
That, silenced by my advent, finds once more,
After an interval, his instrument,
And tries once—twice—and thrice if I be there;
And on the worn book of old-golden song
I brought not here to read, it seems, but hold
And freshen in this air of withering sweetness;
But on the memory of one absent most,
For whom these lines when they shall greet her eye.

IN A VALE

When I was young, we dwelt in a vale
    By a misty fen that rang all night,
And thus it was the maidens pale
I knew so well, whose garments trail
    Across the reeds to a window light.

The fen had every kind of bloom,
    And for every kind there was a face,
And a voice that has sounded in my room
Across the sill from the outer gloom.
    Each came singly unto her place,

But all came every night with the mist;
    And often they brought so much to say
Of things of moment to which, they wist,
One so lonely was fain to list,
    That the stars were almost faded away

Before the last went, heavy with dew,
    Back to the place from which she came—
Where the bird was before it flew,
Where the flower was before it grew,
    Where bird and flower were one and the same.

And thus it is I know so well
    Why the flower has odor, the bird has song.
You have only to ask me, and I can tell.
No, not vainly there did I dwell,
    Nor vainly listen all the night long.

A DREAM PANG

I had withdrawn in forest, and my song
Was swallowed up in leaves that blew alway;
And to the forest edge you came one day
(This was my dream) and looked and pondered long,
But did not enter, though the wish was strong:
You shook your pensive head as who should say,
"I dare not—too far in his footsteps stray—
He must seek me would he undo the wrong."

Not far, but near, I stood and saw it all
Behind low boughs the trees let down outside;
And the sweet pang it cost me not to call
And tell you that I saw does still abide.
But 'tis not true that thus I dwelt aloof,
For the wood wakes, and you are here for proof.

IN NEGLECT

They leave us so to the way we took,
    As two in whom they were proved mistaken,
That we sit sometimes in the wayside nook,
With mischievous, vagrant, seraphic look,
    And *try* if we cannot feel forsaken.

THE VANTAGE POINT

If tired of trees I seek again mankind,
    Well I know where to hie me—in the dawn,
    To a slope where the cattle keep the lawn.
There amid lolling juniper reclined,
Myself unseen, I see in white defined
    Far off the homes of men, and farther still,
    The graves of men on an opposing hill,
Living or dead, whichever are to mind.

And if by noon I have too much of these,
    I have but to turn on my arm, and lo,
    The sun-burned hillside sets my face aglow,
My breathing shakes the bluet like a breeze,
    I smell the earth, I smell the bruisèd plant,
    I look into the crater of the ant.

MOWING

There was never a sound beside the wood but
    one,
And that was my long scythe whispering to
    the ground.
What was it it whispered? I knew not well
    myself;
Perhaps it was something about the heat of
    the sun,
Something, perhaps, about the lack of sound—
And that was why it whispered and did not
    speak.
It was no dream of the gift of idle hours,
Or easy gold at the hand of fay or elf:
Anything more than the truth would have
    seemed too weak
To the earnest love that laid the swale in
    rows,
Not without feeble-pointed spikes of flowers
(Pale orchises), and scared a bright green
    snake.
The fact is the sweetest dream that labor
    knows.
My long scythe whispered and left the hay to
    make.

GOING FOR WATER

The well was dry beside the door,
    And so we went with pail and can
Across the fields behind the house
    To seek the brook if still it ran;

Not loth to have excuse to go,
    Because the autumn eve was fair
(Though chill), because the fields were ours,
    And by the brook our woods were there.

We ran as if to meet the moon
    That slowly dawned behind the trees,
The barren boughs without the leaves,
    Without the birds, without the breeze.

But once within the wood, we paused
    Like gnomes that hid us from the moon,
Ready to run to hiding new
    With laughter when she found us soon.

Each laid on other a staying hand
    To listen ere we dared to look,
And in the hush we joined to make
    We heard, we knew we heard the brook.

A note as from a single place,
    A slender tinkling fall that made
Now drops that floated on the pool
    Like pearls, and now a silver blade.

THE TRIAL BY EXISTENCE

Even the bravest that are slain
   Shall not dissemble their surprise
On waking to find valor reign,
   Even as on earth, in paradise;
And where they sought without the sword
   Wide fields of asphodel fore'er,
To find that the utmost reward
   Of daring should be still to dare.

The light of heaven falls whole and white
   And is not shattered into dyes,
The light for ever is morning light;
   The hills are verdured pasture-wise;
The angel hosts with freshness go,
   And seek with laughter what to brave;—
And binding all is the hushed snow
   Of the far-distant breaking wave.

And from a cliff-top is proclaimed
   The gathering of the souls for birth,
The trial by existence named,
   The obscuration upon earth.
And the slant spirits trooping by
   In streams and cross- and counter-streams
Can but give ear to that sweet cry
   For its suggestion of what dreams!

And the more loitering are turned
   To view once more the sacrifice
Of those who for some good discerned
   Will gladly give up paradise.
And a white shimmering concourse rolls
   Toward the throne to witness there
The speeding of devoted souls
   Which God makes his especial care.

And none are taken but who will,
   Having first heard the life read out
That opens earthward, good and ill,
   Beyond the shadow of a doubt;
And very beautifully God limns,
   And tenderly, life's little dream,
But naught extenuates or dims,
   Setting the thing that is supreme.

Nor is there wanting in the press
   Some spirit to stand simply forth,
Heroic in its nakedness,
   Against the uttermost of earth.
The tale of earth's unhonored things
   Sounds nobler there than 'neath the sun;
And the mind whirls and the heart sings,
   And a shout greets the daring one.

But always God speaks at the end:
   "One thought in agony of strife
The bravest would have by for friend,
   The memory that he chose the life;
But the pure fate to which you go
   Admits no memory of choice,
Or the woe were not earthly woe
   To which you give the assenting voice."

And so the choice must be again,
　But the last choice is still the same;
And the awe passes wonder then,
　And a hush falls for all acclaim.
And God has taken a flower of gold
　And broken it, and used therefrom
The mystic link to bind and hold
　Spirit to matter till death come.

'Tis of the essence of life here,
　Though we choose greatly, still to lack
The lasting memory at all clear,
　That life has for us on the wrack
Nothing but what we somehow chose;
　Thus are we wholly stripped of pride
In the pain that has but one close,
　Bearing it crushed and mystified.

IN EQUAL SACRIFICE

Thus of old the Douglas did:
He left his land as he was bid
With the royal heart of Robert the Bruce
In a golden case with a golden lid,

To carry the same to the Holy Land;
By which we see and understand
That that was the place to carry a heart
At loyalty and love's command,

And that was the case to carry it in.
The Douglas had not far to win
Before he came to the land of Spain,
Where long a holy war had been

Against the too-victorious Moor;
And there his courage could not endure
Not to strike a blow for God
Before he made his errand sure.

And ever it was intended so,
That a man for God should strike a blow,
No matter the heart he has in charge
For the Holy Land where hearts should go.

But when in battle the foe were met,
The Douglas found him sore beset,
With only strength of the fighting arm
For one more battle passage yet—

And that as vain to save the day
As bring his body safe away—
Only a signal deed to do
And a last sounding word to say.

The heart he wore in a golden chain
He swung and flung forth into the plain,
And followed it crying "Heart or death!"
And fighting over it perished fain.

So may another do of right,
Give a heart to the hopeless fight,
The more of right the more he loves;
So may another redouble might

For a few swift gleams of the angry brand,
Scorning greatly not to demand
In equal sacrifice with his
The heart he bore to the Holy Land.

THE TUFT OF FLOWERS

I went to turn the grass once after one
Who mowed it in the dew before the sun.

The dew was gone that made his blade so keen
Before I came to view the levelled scene.

I looked for him behind an isle of trees;
I listened for his whetstone on the breeze.

But he had gone his way, the grass all mown,
And I must be, as he had been,—alone,

"As all must be," I said within my heart,
"Whether they work together or apart."

But as I said it, swift there passed me by
On noiseless wing a 'wildered butterfly,

Seeking with memories grown dim o'er night
Some resting flower of yesterday's delight.

And once I marked his flight go round and round,
As where some flower lay withering on the ground.

And then he flew as far as eye could see,
And then on tremulous wing came back to me.

I thought of questions that have no reply,
And would have turned to toss the grass to dry;

But he turned first, and led my eye to look
At a tall tuft of flowers beside a brook,

A leaping tongue of bloom the scythe had spared
Beside a reedy brook the scythe had bared.

I left my place to know them by their name,
Finding them butterfly weed when I came.

The mower in the dew had loved them thus,
By leaving them to flourish, not for us,

Nor yet to draw one thought of ours to him.
But from sheer morning gladness at the brim.

The butterfly and I had lit upon,
Nevertheless, a message from the dawn,

That made me hear the wakening birds around,
And hear his long scythe whispering to the ground,

And feel a spirit kindred to my own;
So that henceforth I worked no more alone;

But glad with him, I worked as with his aid,
And weary, sought at noon with him the shade;

And dreaming, as it were, held brotherly speech
With one whose thought I had not hoped to reach.

"Men work together," I told him from the heart,
"Whether they work together or apart."

SPOILS OF THE DEAD

Two fairies it was
  On a still summer day
Came forth in the woods
  With the flowers to play.

The flowers they plucked
  They cast on the ground
For others, and those
  For still others they found.

Flower-guided it was
  That they came as they ran
On something that lay
  In the shape of a man.

The snow must have made
  The feathery bed
When this one fell
  On the sleep of the dead.

But the snow was gone
  A long time ago,
And the body he wore
  Nigh gone with the snow.

The fairies drew near
  And keenly espied
A ring on his hand
  And a chain at his side.

They knelt in the leaves
    And eerily played
With the glittering things,
    And were not afraid.

And when they went home
    To hide in their burrow,
They took them along
    To play with tomorrow.

When *you* came on death,
    Did you not come flower-guided
Like the elves in the wood?
    I remember that I did.

But I recognized death
    With sorrow and dread,
And I hated and hate
    The spoils of the dead.

PAN WITH US

Pan came out of the woods one day,—
His skin and his hair and his eyes were gray,
The gray of the moss of walls were they,—
   And stood in the sun and looked his fill
   At wooded valley and wooded hill.

He stood in the zephyr, pipes in hand,
On a height of naked pasture land;
In all the country he did command
   He saw no smoke and he saw no roof.
   That was well! and he stamped a hoof.

His heart knew peace, for none came here
To this lean feeding save once a year
Someone to salt the half-wild steer,
   Or homespun children with clicking pails
   Who see so little they tell no tales.

He tossed his pipes, too hard to teach
A new-world song, far out of reach,
For a sylvan sign that the blue jay's screech
   And the whimper of hawks beside the sun
   Were music enough for him, for one.

Times were changed from what they were:
Such pipes kept less of power to stir
The fruited bough of the juniper
   And the fragile bluets clustered there
   Than the merest aimless breath of air.

They were pipes of pagan mirth,
And the world had found new terms of worth.
He laid him down on the sunburned earth
   And ravelled a flower and looked away—
   Play? Play?—What should he play?

REVELATION

We make ourselves a place apart
   Behind light words that tease and flout,
But oh, the agitated heart
   Till someone find us really out.

'Tis pity if the case require
   (Or so we say) that in the end
We speak the literal to inspire
   The understanding of a friend.

But so with all, from babes that play
   At hide-and-seek to God afar,
So all who hide too well away
   Must speak and tell us where they are.

THE DEMIURGE'S LAUGH

It was far in the sameness of the wood;
   I was running with joy on the Demon's trail,
Though I knew what I hunted was no true god.
   It was just as the light was beginning to fail
That I suddenly heard—all I needed to hear:
It has lasted me many and many a year.

The sound was behind me instead of before,
   A sleepy sound, but mocking half,
As of one who utterly couldn't care.
   The Demon arose from his swallow to laugh,
Brushing the dirt from his eye as he went;
And well I knew what the Demon meant.

I shall not forget how his laugh rang out.
   I felt as a fool to have been so caught,
And checked my steps to make pretence
   It was something among the leaves I sought
(Though doubtful whether he stayed to see).
Thereafter I sat me against a tree.

A LINE-STORM SONG

The line-storm clouds fly tattered and swift,
  The road is forlorn all day,
Where a myriad snowy quartz stones lift,
  And the hoofprints vanish away.
The roadside flowers, too wet for the bee,
  Expend their bloom in vain.
Come over the hills and far with me,
  And be my love in the rain.

The birds have less to say for themselves
  In the wood-world's torn despair
Than now these numberless years the elves,
  Although they are no less there:
All song of the woods is crushed like some
  Wild, easily shattered rose.
Come, be my love in the wet woods; come,
  Where the boughs rain when it blows.

There is the gale to urge behind
  And bruit our singing down,
And the shallow waters aflutter with wind
  From which to gather your gown.
What matter if we go clear to the west,
  And come not through dry-shod?
For wilding brooch shall wet your breast
  The rain-fresh goldenrod.

Oh, never this whelming east wind swells
    But it seems like the sea's return
To the ancient lands where it left the shells
    Before the age of the fern;
And it seems like the time when after doubt
    Our love came back amain.
Oh, come forth into the storm and rout
    And be my love in the rain.

NOW CLOSE THE WINDOWS

Now close the windows and hush all the fields;
   If the trees must, let them silently toss;
No bird is singing now, and if there is,
   Be it my loss.

It will be long ere the marshes resume,
   It will be long ere the earliest bird:
So close the windows and not hear the wind,
   But see all wind-stirred.

OCTOBER

O hushed October morning mild,
Thy leaves have ripened to the fall;
Tomorrow's wind, if it be wild,
Should waste them all.
The crows above the forest call;
Tomorrow they may form and go.
O hushed October morning mild,
Begin the hours of this day slow,
Make the day seem to us less brief.
Hearts not averse to being beguiled,
Beguile us in the way you know;
Release one leaf at break of day;
At noon release another leaf;
One from our trees, one far away;
Retard the sun with gentle mist;
Enchant the land with amethyst.
Slow, slow!
For the grapes' sake, if they were all,
Whose leaves already are burnt with frost,
Whose clustered fruit must else be lost—
For the grapes' sake along the wall.

MY BUTTERFLY

Thine emulous fond flowers are dead, too,
And the daft sun-assaulter, he
That frighted thee so oft, is fled or dead:
Save only me
(Nor is it sad to thee!)
Save only me
There is none left to mourn thee in the fields.

The gray grass is not dappled with the snow;
Its two banks have not shut upon the river;
But it is long ago—
It seems forever—
Since first I saw thee glance,
With all the dazzling other ones,
In airy dalliance,
Precipitate in love,
Tossed, tangled, whirled and whirled above,
Like a limp rose wreath in a fairy dance.

When that was, the soft mist
Of my regret hung not on all the land,
And I was glad for thee,
And glad for me, I wist.

Thou didst not know, who tottered, wandering on high,
That fate had made thee for the pleasure of the wind,
With those great careless wings,
Nor yet did I.

And there were other things:
It seemed God let thee flutter from his gentle clasp:
Then fearful he had let thee win
Too far beyond him to be gathered in,
Snatched thee, o'er eager, with ungentle grasp.

Ah! I remember me
How once conspiracy was rife
Against my life—
The languor of it and the dreaming fond;
Surging, the grasses dizzied me of thought,
The breeze three odors brought,
And a gem-flower waved in a wand!

Then when I was distraught
And could not speak,
Sidelong, full on my cheek,
What should that reckless zephyr fling
But the wild touch of thy dye-dusty wing!

I found that wing broken today!
For thou art dead, I said,
And the strange birds say.
I found it with the withered leaves
Under the eaves.

RELUCTANCE

Out through the fields and the woods
   And over the walls I have wended;
I have climbed the hills of view
   And looked at the world, and descended;
I have come by the highway home,
   And lo, it is ended.

The leaves are all dead on the ground,
   Save those that the oak is keeping
To ravel them one by one
   And let them go scraping and creeping
Out over the crusted snow,
   When others are sleeping.

And the dead leaves lie huddled and still,
   No longer blown hither and thither;
The last lone aster is gone;
   The flowers of the witch hazel wither;
The heart is still aching to seek,
   But the feet question "Whither?"

Ah, when to the heart of man
   Was it ever less than a treason
To go with the drift of things,
   To yield with a grace to reason,
And bow and accept the end
   Of a love or a season?

North of Boston

THE PASTURE

I'm going out to clean the pasture spring;
I'll only stop to rake the leaves away
(And wait to watch the water clear, I may):
I sha'n't be gone long.—You come too.

I'm going out to fetch the little calf
That's standing by the mother. It's so young,
It totters when she licks it with her tongue.
I sha'n't be gone long.—You come too.

Mending Wall takes up the theme where
A Tuft of Flowers in *A Boy's Will*
laid it down.

MENDING WALL

Something there is that doesn't love a wall,
That sends the frozen-ground-swell under it,
And spills the upper boulders in the sun;
And makes gaps even two can pass abreast.
The work of hunters is another thing:
I have come after them and made repair
Where they have left not one stone on a stone,
But they would have the rabbit out of hiding,
To please the yelping dogs. The gaps I mean,
No one has seen them made or heard them made,
But at spring mending-time we find them there.
I let my neighbor know beyond the hill;
And on a day we meet to walk the line
And set the wall between us once again.
We keep the wall between us as we go.
To each the boulders that have fallen to each.
And some are loaves and some so nearly balls
We have to use a spell to make them balance:
"Stay where you are until our backs are turned!"
We wear our fingers rough with handling them.
Oh, just another kind of outdoor game,
One on a side. It comes to little more:
There where it is we do not need the wall:
He is all pine and I am apple orchard.
My apple trees will never get across
And eat the cones under his pines, I tell him.
He only says, "Good fences make good neighbors."
Spring is the mischief in me, and I wonder
If I could put a notion in his head:
"*Why* do they make good neighbors? Isn't it
Where there are cows? But here there are no cows.

Before I built a wall I'd ask to know
What I was walling in or walling out,
And to whom I was like to give offense.
Something there is that doesn't love a wall,
That wants it down." I could say "Elves" to him,
But it's not elves exactly, and I'd rather
He said it for himself. I see him there
Bringing a stone grasped firmly by the top
In each hand, like an old-stone savage armed.
He moves in darkness as it seems to me,
Not of woods only and the shade of trees.
He will not go behind his father's saying,
And he likes having thought of it so well
He says again, "Good fences make good neighbors."

THE DEATH OF THE HIRED MAN

Mary sat musing on the lamp flame at the table
Waiting for Warren. When she heard his step,
She ran on tiptoe down the darkened passage
To meet him in the doorway with the news
And put him on his guard. "Silas is back."
She pushed him outward with her through the door
And shut it after her. "Be kind," she said.
She took the market things from Warren's arms
And set them on the porch, then drew him down
To sit beside her on the wooden steps.

"When was I ever anything but kind to him?
But I'll not have the fellow back," he said.
"I told him so last haying, didn't I?
'If he left then,' I said, 'that ended it.'
What good is he? Who else will harbor him
At his age for the little he can do?
What help he is there's no depending on.
Off he goes always when I need him most.
'He thinks he ought to earn a little pay,
Enough at least to buy tobacco with,
So he won't have to beg and be beholden.'
'All right,' I say, 'I can't afford to pay
Any fixed wages, though I wish I could.'
'Someone else can.' 'Then someone else will have to.'
I shouldn't mind his bettering himself
If that was what it was. You can be certain,
When he begins like that, there's someone at him
Trying to coax him off with pocket money,—
In haying time, when any help is scarce.
In winter he comes back to us. I'm done."

"Sh! not so loud: he'll hear you," Mary said.

"I want him to: he'll have to soon or late."

"He's worn out. He's asleep beside the stove.
When I came up from Rowe's I found him here,
Huddled against the barn door fast asleep,
A miserable sight, and frightening, too—
You needn't smile—I didn't recognize him—
I wasn't looking for him—and he's changed.
Wait till you see."

                    "Where did you say he'd been?"

"He didn't say. I dragged him to the house,
And gave him tea and tried to make him smoke.
I tried to make him talk about his travels.
Nothing would do: he just kept nodding off."

"What did he say? Did he say anything?"

"But little."

                    "Anything? Mary, confess
He said he'd come to ditch the meadow for me."

"Warren!"

                    "But did he? I just want to know."

"Of course he did. What would you have him say?
Surely you wouldn't grudge the poor old man
Some humble way to save his self-respect.
He added, if you really care to know,
He meant to clear the upper pasture, too.
That sounds like something you have heard before?

Warren, I wish you could have heard the way
He jumbled everything. I stopped to look
Two or three times—he made me feel so queer—
To see if he was talking in his sleep.
He ran on Harold Wilson—you remember—
The boy you had in haying four years since.
He's finished school, and teaching in his college.
Silas declares you'll have to get him back.
He says they two will make a team for work:
Between them they will lay this farm as smooth!
The way he mixed that in with other things.
He thinks young Wilson a likely lad, though daft
On education—you know how they fought
All through July under the blazing sun,
Silas up on the cart to build the load,
Harold along beside to pitch it on.''

"Yes, I took care to keep well out of earshot."

"Well, those days trouble Silas like a dream.
You wouldn't think they would. How some things
        linger!
Harold's young college boy's assurance piqued him.
After so many years he still keeps finding
Good arguments he sees he might have used.
I sympathize. I know just how it feels
To think of the right thing to say too late.
Harold's associated in his mind with Latin.
He asked me what I thought of Harold's saying
He studied Latin like the violin
Because he liked it—that an argument!
He said he couldn't make the boy believe
He could find water with a hazel prong—
Which showed how much good school had ever
        done him.
He wanted to go over that. But most of all

He thinks if he could have another chance
To teach him how to build a load of hay——"

"I know, that's Silas' one accomplishment.
He bundles every forkful in its place,
And tags and numbers it for future reference,
So he can find and easily dislodge it
In the unloading. Silas does that well.
He takes it out in bunches like big birds' nests.
You never see him standing on the hay
He's trying to lift, straining to lift himself."

"He thinks if he could teach him that, he'd be
Some good perhaps to someone in the world.
He hates to see a boy the fool of books.
Poor Silas, so concerned for other folk,
And nothing to look backward to with pride,
And nothing to look forward to with hope,
So now and never any different."

Part of a moon was falling down the west,
Dragging the whole sky with it to the hills.
Its light poured softly in her lap. She saw
And spread her apron to it. She put out her hand
Among the harp-like morning-glory strings,
Taut with the dew from garden bed to eaves,
As if she played unheard the tenderness
That wrought on him beside her in the night.
"Warren," she said, "he has come home to die:
You needn't be afraid he'll leave you this time."

"Home," he mocked gently.

                              "Yes, what else but home?
It all depends on what you mean by home.
Of course he's nothing to us, any more

Than was the hound that came a stranger to us
Out of the woods, worn out upon the trail."

"Home is the place where, when you have to go
        there,
They have to take you in."

                        "I should have called it
Something you somehow haven't to deserve."

Warren leaned out and took a step or two,
Picked up a little stick, and brought it back
And broke it in his hand and tossed it by.
"Silas has better claim on us you think
Than on his brother? Thirteen little miles
As the road winds would bring him to his door.
Silas has walked that far no doubt today.
Why didn't he go there? His brother's rich,
A somebody—director in the bank."

"He never told us that."

                        "We know it though."

"I think his brother ought to help, of course.
I'll see to that if there is need. He ought of right
To take him in, and might be willing to—
He may be better than appearances.
But have some pity on Silas. Do you think
If he'd had any pride in claiming kin
Or anything he looked for from his brother,
He'd keep so still about him all this time?"

"I wonder what's between them."

                        "I can tell you.
Silas is what he is—we wouldn't mind him—
But just the kind that kinsfolk can't abide.

He never did a thing so very bad.
He don't know why he isn't quite as good
As anyone. He won't be made ashamed
To please his brother, worthless though he is."

"*I* can't think Si ever hurt anyone."

"No, but he hurt my heart the way he lay
And rolled his old head on that sharp-edged chair-
         back.
He wouldn't let me put him on the lounge.
You must go in and see what you can do.
I made the bed up for him there tonight.
You'll be surprised at him—how much he's broken.
His working days are done; I'm sure of it."

"I'd not be in a hurry to say that."

"I haven't been. Go, look, see for yourself.
But, Warren, please remember how it is:
He's come to help you ditch the meadow.
He has a plan. You mustn't laugh at him.
He may not speak of it, and then he may.
I'll sit and see if that small sailing cloud
Will hit or miss the moon."

                              It hit the moon.
Then there were three there, making a dim row,
The moon, the little silver cloud, and she.
Warren returned—too soon, it seemed to her,
Slipped to her side, caught up her hand and waited.

"Warren," she questioned.

                    "Dead," was all he answered.

THE MOUNTAIN

The mountain held the town as in a shadow
I saw so much before I slept there once:
I noticed that I missed stars in the west,
Where its black body cut into the sky.
Near me it seemed: I felt it like a wall
Behind which I was sheltered from a wind.
And yet between the town and it I found,
When I walked forth at dawn to see new things,
Were fields, a river, and beyond, more fields.
The river at the time was fallen away,
And made a widespread brawl on cobblestones;
But the signs showed what it had done in spring;
Good grassland gullied out, and in the grass
Ridges of sand, and driftwood stripped of bark.
I crossed the river and swung round the mountain.
And there I met a man who moved so slow
With white-faced oxen in a heavy cart,
It seemed no harm to stop him altogether.

"What town is this?" I asked.

                              "This? Lunenburg."

Then I was wrong: the town of my sojourn,
Beyond the bridge, was not that of the mountain,
But only felt at night its shadowy presence.
"Where is your village? Very far from here?"

"There is no village—only scattered farms.
We were but sixty voters last election.
We can't in nature grow to many more:
That thing takes all the room!" He moved his goad.

The mountain stood there to be pointed at.
Pasture ran up the side a little way,
And then there was a wall of trees with trunks:
After that only tops of trees, and cliffs
Imperfectly concealed among the leaves.
A dry ravine emerged from under boughs
Into the pasture.

                              "That looks like a path.
Is that the way to reach the top from here?—
Not for this morning, but some other time:
I must be getting back to breakfast now."

"I don't advise your trying from this side.
There is no proper path, but those that *have*
Been up, I understand, have climbed from Ladd's.
That's five miles back. You can't mistake the place:
They logged it there last winter some way up.
I'd take you, but I'm bound the other way."

"You've never climbed it?"

                              "I've been on the sides
Deer-hunting and trout-fishing. There's a brook
That starts up on it somewhere—I've heard say
Right on the top, tip-top—a curious thing.
But what would interest you about the brook,
It's always cold in summer, warm in winter.
One of the great sights going is to see
It steam in winter like an ox's breath,
Until the bushes all along its banks
Are inch-deep with the frosty spines and bristles—
You know the kind. Then let the sun shine on it!"

"There ought to be a view around the world
From such a mountain—if it isn't wooded
Clear to the top." I saw through leafy screens

Great granite terraces in sun and shadow,
Shelves one could rest a knee on getting up—
With depths behind him sheer a hundred feet;
Or turn and sit on and look out and down,
With little ferns in crevices at his elbow.

"As to that I can't say. But there's the spring,
Right on the summit, almost like a fountain.
That ought to be worth seeing."

                                    "If it's there.
You never saw it?"

                        "I guess there's no doubt
About its being there. I never saw it.
It may not be right on the very top:
It wouldn't have to be a long way down
To have some head of water from above,
And a *good distance* down might not be noticed
By anyone who'd come a long way up.
One time I asked a fellow climbing it
To look and tell me later how it was."

"What did he say?"

                        "He said there was a lake
Somewhere in Ireland on a mountain top."

"But a lake's different. What about the spring?"

"He never got up high enough to see.
That's why I don't advise your trying this side.
He tried this side. I've always meant to go
And look myself, but you know how it is:
It doesn't seem so much to climb a mountain
You've worked around the foot of all your life.

What would I do? Go in my overalls,
With a big stick, the same as when the cows
Haven't come down to the bars at milking time?
Or with a shotgun for a stray black bear?
'Twouldn't seem real to climb for climbing it."
"I shouldn't climb it if I didn't want to—
Not for the sake of climbing. What's its name?"

"We call it Hor: I don't know if that's right."

"Can one walk around it? Would it be too far?"

"You can drive round and keep in Lunenburg,
But it's as much as ever you can do,
The boundary lines keep in so close to it.
Hor is the township, and the township's Hor—
And a few houses sprinkled round the foot,
Like boulders broken off the upper cliff,
Rolled out a little farther than the rest."

"Warm in December, cold in June, you say?"

"I don't suppose the water's changed at all.
You and I know enough to know it's warm
Compared with cold, and cold compared with warm.
But all the fun's in how you say a thing."

"You've lived here all your life?"

                                    "Ever since Hor
Was no bigger than a——" What, I did not hear.
He drew the oxen toward him with light touches
Of his slim goad on nose and offside flank,
Gave them their marching orders and was moving.

A HUNDRED COLLARS

Lancaster bore him—such a little town,
Such a great man. It doesn't see him often
Of late years, though he keeps the old homestead
And sends the children down there with their mother
To run wild in the summer—a little wild.
Sometimes he joins them for a day or two
And sees old friends he somehow can't get near.
They meet him in the general store at night,
Preoccupied with formidable mail,
Riffling a printed letter as he talks.
They seem afraid. He wouldn't have it so:
Though a great scholar, he's a democrat,
If not at heart, at least on principle.
Lately when coming up to Lancaster
His train being late he missed another train
And had four hours to wait at Woodsville Junction
After eleven o'clock at night. Too tired
To think of sitting such an ordeal out,
He turned to the hotel to find a bed.

"No room," the night clerk said. "Unless——"
Woodsville's a place of shrieks and wandering lamps
And cars that shook and rattle—and *one* hotel.

"You say 'unless.' "

                    "Unless you wouldn't mind
Sharing a room with someone else."

                              "Who is it?"

"A man."

"So I should hope. What kind of man?"

"I know him: he's all right. A man's a man.
Separate beds of course you understand."
The night clerk blinked his eyes and dared him on.

"Who's that man sleeping in the office chair?
Has he had the refusal of my chance?"

"He was afraid of being robbed or murdered.
What do you say?"

                    "I'll have to have a bed."

The night clerk led him up three flights of stairs
And down a narrow passage full of doors,
At the last one of which he knocked and entered.
"Lafe, here's a fellow wants to share your room."

"Show him this way. I'm not afraid of him.
I'm not so drunk I can't take care of myself."

The night clerk clapped a bedstead on the foot.
"This will be yours. Good night," he said, and went.

"Lafe was the name, I think?"

                        "Yes, Layfayette.
You got it the first time. And yours?"

                          "Magoon.
Doctor Magoon."

              "A Doctor?"

                  "Well, a teacher."

"Professor Square-the-circle-till-you're-tired?
Hold on, there's something I don't think of now
That I had on my mind to ask the first
Man that knew anything I happened in with.
I'll ask you later—don't let me forget it."

The Doctor looked at Lafe and looked away.
A man? A brute. Naked above the waist,
He sat there creased and shining in the light,
Fumbling the buttons in a well-starched shirt.
"I'm moving into a size-larger shirt.
I've felt mean lately; mean's no name for it.
I just found what the matter was tonight:
I've been a-choking like a nursery tree
When it outgrows the wire band of its name tag.
I blamed it on the hot spell we've been having.
'Twas nothing but my foolish hanging back,
Not liking to own up I'd grown a size.
Number eighteen this is. What size do you wear?"

The Doctor caught his throat convulsively.
"Oh—ah—fourteen—fourteen."

                    "Fourteen! You say so!
I can remember when I wore fourteen.
And come to think I must have back at home
More than a hundred collars, size fourteen.
Too bad to waste them all. You ought to have them.
They're yours and welcome; let me send them to you.
What makes you stand there on one leg like that?
You're not much furtherer than where Kike left you.
You act as if you wished you hadn't come.
Sit down or lie down, friend; you make me nervous."

The Doctor made a subdued dash for it,
And propped himself at bay against a pillow.

"Not that way, with your shoes on Kike's white bed.
You can't rest that way. Let me pull your shoes off."

"Don't touch me, please—I say, don't touch me, please.
I'll not be put to bed by you, my man."

"Just as you say. Have it your own way then.
'My man' is it? You talk like a professor.
Speaking of who's afraid of who, however,
I'm thinking I have more to lose than you
If anything should happen to be wrong.
Who wants to cut your number fourteen throat!
Let's have a show down as an evidence
Of good faith. There is ninety dollars.
Come, if you're not afraid."

                              "*I*'m not afraid.
There's five: that's all I carry."

                              "I can search you?
Where are you moving over to? Stay still.
You'd better tuck your money under you
And sleep on it the way I always do
When I'm with people I don't trust at night."

"Will you believe me if I put it there
Right on the counterpane—that I do trust you?"

"You'd say so, Mister Man.—I'm a collector.
My ninety isn't mine—you won't think that.
I pick it up a dollar at a time
All round the country for the *Weekly News*,
Published in Bow. You know the *Weekly News*?"

"Known it since I was young."

                              "Then you know me.

Now we are getting on together—talking.
I'm sort of Something for it at the front.
My business is to find what people want:
They pay for it, and so they ought to have it.
Fairbanks, he says to me—he's editor—
Feel out the public sentiment—he says.
A good deal comes on me when all is said.
The only trouble is we disagree
In politics: I'm Vermont Democrat—
You know what that is, sort of double-dyed;
The *News* has always been Republican.
Fairbanks, he says to me, 'Help us this year,'
Meaning by us their ticket. 'No,' I says,
'I can't and won't. You've been in long enough:
It's time you turned around and boosted us.
You'll have to pay me more than ten a week
If I'm expected to elect Bill Taft.
I doubt if I could do it anyway.' "

"You seem to shape the paper's policy."

"You see I'm in with everybody, know 'em all.
I almost know their farms as well as they do."

"You drive around? It must be pleasant work."

"It's business, but I can't say it's not fun.
What I like best's the lay of different farms,
Coming out on them from a stretch of woods,
Or over a hill or round a sudden corner.
I like to find folks getting out in spring,
Raking the dooryard, working near the house.
Later they get out further in the fields.
Everything's shut sometimes except the barn;
The family's all away in some back meadow.
There's a hay load a-coming—when it comes.

And later still they all get driven in:
The fields are stripped to lawn, the garden patches
Stripped to bare ground, the apple trees
To whips and poles. There's nobody about.
The chimney, though, keeps up a good brisk smoking.
And I lie back and ride. I take the reins
Only when someone's coming, and the mare
Stops when she likes: I tell her when to go.
I've spoiled Jemima in more ways than one.
She's got so she turns in at every house
As if she had some sort of curvature,
No matter if I have no errand there.
She thinks I'm sociable. I maybe am.
It's seldom I get down except for meals, though.
Folks entertain me from the kitchen doorstep,
All in a family row down to the youngest."

"One would suppose they might not be as glad
To see you as you are to see them."

                                                "Oh,

Because I want their dollar. I don't want
Anything they've not got. I never dun.
I'm there, and they can pay me if they like.
I go nowhere on purpose: I happen by.
Sorry there is no cup to give you a drink.
I drink out of the bottle—not your style.
Mayn't I offer you——?"

                              "No, no, no, thank you."

"Just as you say. Here's looking at you then.—
And now I'm leaving you a little while.

You'll rest easier when I'm gone, perhaps—
Lie down—let yourself go and get some sleep.
But first—let's see—what was I going to ask you?
Those collars—who shall I address them to,
Suppose you aren't awake when I come back?"

"Really, friend, I can't let you. You—may need them."

"Not till I shrink, when they'll be out of style."

"But really I—I have so many collars."

"I don't know who I rather would have have them.
They're only turning yellow where they are.
But you're the doctor as the saying is.
I'll put the light out. Don't you wait for me:
I've just begun the night. You get some sleep.
I'll knock so-fashion and peep round the door
When I come back so you'll know who it is.
There's nothing I'm afraid of like scared people.
I don't want you should shoot me in the head.
What am I doing carrying off this bottle?
There now, you get some sleep."

                                He shut the door.
The Doctor slid a little down the pillow.

HOME BURIAL

He saw her from the bottom of the stairs
Before she saw him. She was starting down,
Looking back over her shoulder at some fear.
She took a doubtful step and then undid it
To raise herself and look again. He spoke
Advancing toward her: "What is it you see
From up there always—for I want to know."
She turned and sank upon her skirts at that,
And her face changed from terrified to dull.
He said to gain time: "What is it you see,"
Mounting until she cowered under him.
"I will find out now—you must tell me, dear."
She, in her place, refused him any help
With the least stiffening of her neck and silence.
She let him look, sure that he wouldn't see,
Blind creature; and a while he didn't see.
But at last he murmured, "Oh," and again, "Oh."

"What is it—what?" she said.

                              "Just that I see."

"You don't," she challenged. "Tell me what it is."

"The wonder is I didn't see at once.
I never noticed it from here before.
I must be wonted to it—that's the reason.
The little graveyard where my people are!
So small the window frames the whole of it.
Not so much larger than a bedroom, is it?
There are three stones of slate and one of marble,

Broad-shouldered little slabs there in the sunlight
On the sidehill. We haven't to mind *those*.
But I understand: it is not the stones,
But the child's mound——"

                    "Don't, don't, don't, don't," she cried.

She withdrew shrinking from beneath his arm
That rested on the banister, and slid downstairs;
And turned on him with such a daunting look,
He said twice over before he knew himself:
"Can't a man speak of his own child he's lost?"

"Not you! Oh, where's my hat? Oh, I don't need it!
I must get out of here. I must get air.
I don't know rightly whether any man can."

"Amy! Don't go to someone else this time.
Listen to me. I won't come down the stairs."
He sat and fixed his chin between his fists.
"There's something I should like to ask you, dear."

"You don't know how to ask it."

                              "Help me, then."
Her fingers moved the latch for all reply.

"My words are nearly always an offence.
I don't know how to speak of anything
So as to please you. But I might be taught
I should suppose. I can't say I see how.
A man must partly give up being a man
With womenfolk. We could have some arrangement
By which I'd bind myself to keep hands off
Anything special you're a-mind to name.
Though I don't like such things 'twixt those that love.

Two that don't love can't live together without them.
But two that do can't live together with them."
She moved the latch a little. "Don't—don't go.
Don't carry it to someone else this time.
Tell me about it if it's something human.
Let me into your grief. I'm not so much
Unlike other folks as your standing there
Apart would make me out. Give me my chance.
I do think, though, you overdo it a little.
What was it brought you up to think it the thing
To take your mother-loss of a first child
So inconsolably—in the face of love.
You'd think his memory might be satisfied——"

"There you go sneering now!"

                                    "I'm not, I'm not!
You make me angry. I'll come down to you.
God, what a woman! And it's come to this,
A man can't speak of his own child that's dead."

"You can't because you don't know how.
If you had any feelings, you that dug
With your own hand—how could you?—his little grave;
I saw you from that very window there,
Making the gravel leap and leap in air,
Leap up, like that, like that, and land so lightly
And roll back down the mound beside the hole.
I thought, Who is that man? I didn't know you.
And I crept down the stairs and up the stairs
To look again, and still your spade kept lifting.
Then you came in. I heard your rumbling voice
Out in the kitchen, and I don't know why,
But I went near to see with my own eyes.
You could sit there with the stains on your shoes
Of the fresh earth from your own baby's grave

And talk about your everyday concerns.
You had stood the spade up against the wall
Outside there in the entry, for I saw it."

"I shall laugh the worst laugh I ever laughed.
I'm cursed. God, if I don't believe I'm cursed."

"I can repeat the very words you were saying.
'Three foggy mornings and one rainy day
Will rot the best birch fence a man can build.'
Think of it, talk like that at such a time!
What had how long it takes a birch to rot
To do with what was in the darkened parlor.
You *couldn't* care! The nearest friends can go
With anyone to death, comes so far short
They might as well not try to go at all.
No, from the time when one is sick to death,
One is alone, and he dies more alone.
Friends make pretence of following to the grave,
But before one is in it, their minds are turned
And making the best of their way back to life
And living people, and things they understand.
But the world's evil. I won't have grief so
If I can change it. Oh, I won't, I won't!"

"There, you have said it all and you feel better.
You won't go now. You're crying. Close the door.
The heart's gone out of it: why keep it up.
Amy! There's someone coming down the road!"

"*You*—oh, you think the talk is all. I must go—
Somewhere out of this house. How can I make you——"

"If—you—do!" She was opening the door wider.
"Where do you mean to go? First tell me that.
I'll follow and bring you back by force. I *will!*—"

THE BLACK COTTAGE

We chanced in passing by that afternoon
To catch it in a sort of special picture
Among tar-banded ancient cherry trees,
Set well back from the road in rank lodged grass,
The little cottage we were speaking of,
A front with just a door between two windows,
Fresh painted by the shower a velvet black.
We paused, the minister and I, to look.
He made as if to hold it at arm's length
Or put the leaves aside that framed it in.
"Pretty," he said. "Come in. No one will care."
The path was a vague parting in the grass
That led us to a weathered windowsill.
We pressed our faces to the pane. "You see," he said,
"Everything's as she left it when she died.
Her sons won't sell the house or the things in it.
They say they mean to come and summer here
Where they were boys. They haven't come this year.
They live so far away—one is out west—
It will be hard for them to keep their word.
Anyway they won't have the place disturbed."
A buttoned hair-cloth lounge spread scrolling arms
Under a crayon portrait on the wall
Done sadly from an old daguerreotype.
"That was the father as he went to war.
She always, when she talked about war,
Sooner or later came and leaned, half knelt
Against the lounge beside it, though I doubt
If such unlifelike lines kept power to stir
Anything in her after all the years.
He fell at Gettysburg or Fredericksburg,

I ought to know—it makes a difference which:
Fredericksburg wasn't Gettysburg, of course.
But what I'm getting to is how forsaken
A little cottage this has always seemed;
Since she went more than ever, but before—
I don't mean altogether by the lives
That had gone out of it, the father first,
Then the two sons, till she was left alone.
(Nothing could draw her after those two sons.
She valued the considerate neglect
She had at some cost taught them after years.)
I mean by the world's having passed it by—
As we almost got by this afternoon.
It always seems to me a sort of mark
To measure how far fifty years have brought us.
Why not sit down if you are in no haste?
These doorsteps seldom have a visitor.
The warping boards pull out their own old nails
With none to tread and put them in their place.
She had her own idea of things, the old lady.
And she liked talk. She had seen Garrison
And Whittier, and had her story of them.
One wasn't long in learning that she thought
Whatever else the Civil War was for
It wasn't just to keep the States together,
Nor just to free the slaves, though it did both.
She wouldn't have believed those ends enough
To have given outright for them all she gave.
Her giving somehow touched the principle
That all men are created free and equal.
And to hear her quaint phrases—so removed
From the world's view today of all those things.
That's a hard mystery of Jefferson's.
What did he mean? Of course the easy way
Is to decide it simply isn't true.
It may not be. I heard a fellow say so.

But never mind, the Welshman got it planted
Where it will trouble us a thousand years.
Each age will have to reconsider it.
You couldn't tell her what the West was saying,
And what the South to her serene belief.
She had some art of hearing and yet not
Hearing the latter wisdom of the world.
White was the only race she ever knew.
Black she had scarcely seen, and yellow never.
But how could they be made so very unlike
By the same hand working in the same stuff?
She had supposed the war decided that.
What are you going to do with such a person?
Strange how such innocence gets its own way.
I shouldn't be surprised if in this world
It were the force that would at last prevail.
Do you know but for her there was a time
When to please younger members of the church,
Or rather say non-members in the church,
Whom we all have to think of nowadays,
I would have changed the Creed a very little?
Not that she ever had to ask me not to;
It never got so far as that; but the bare thought
Of her old tremulous bonnet in the pew,
And of her half asleep was too much for me.
Why, I might wake her up and startle her.
It was the words 'descended into Hades'
That seemed too pagan to our liberal youth.
You know they suffered from a general onslaught.
And well, if they weren't true why keep right on
Saying them like the heathen? We could drop them.
Only—there was the bonnet in the pew.
Such a phrase couldn't have meant much to her.
But suppose she had missed it from the Creed
As a child misses the unsaid Good night,
And falls asleep with heartache—how should *I* feel?

I'm just as glad she made me keep hands off,
For, dear me, why abandon a belief
Merely because it ceases to be true.
Cling to it long enough, and not a doubt
It will turn true again, for so it goes.
Most of the change we think we see in life
Is due to truths being in and out of favor.
As I sit here, and oftentimes, I wish
I could be monarch of a desert land
I could devote and dedicate forever
To the truths we keep coming back and back to.
So desert it would have to be, so walled
By mountain ranges half in summer snow,
No one would covet it or think it worth
The pains of conquering to force change on.
Scattered oases where men dwelt, but mostly
Sand dunes held loosely in tamarisk
Blown over and over themselves in idleness.
Sand grains should sugar in the natal dew
The babe born to the desert, the sand storm
Retard mid-waste my cowering caravans—

"There are bees in this wall." He struck the clapboards,
Fierce heads looked out; small bodies pivoted.
We rose to go. Sunset blazed on the windows.

BLUEBERRIES

"You ought to have seen what I saw on my way
To the village, through Mortenson's pasture today:
Blueberries as big as the end of your thumb,
Real sky-blue, and heavy, and ready to drum
In the cavernous pail of the first one to come!
And all ripe together, not some of them green
And some of them ripe! You ought to have seen!"

"I don't know what part of the pasture you mean."

"You know where they cut off the woods—let me see—
It was two years ago—or no!—can it be
No longer than that?—and the following fall
The fire ran and burned it all up but the wall."

"Why, there hasn't been time for the bushes to grow.
That's always the way with the blueberries, though:
There may not have been the ghost of a sign
Of them anywhere under the shade of the pine,
But get the pine out of the way, you may burn
The pasture all over until not a fern
Or grass-blade is left, not to mention a stick,
And presto, they're up all around you as thick
And hard to explain as a conjuror's trick."

"It must be on charcoal they fatten their fruit.
I taste in them sometimes the flavor of soot.
And after all really they're ebony skinned:
The blue's but a mist from the breath of the wind,
A tarnish that goes at a touch of the hand,
And less than the tan with which pickers are tanned."

"Does Mortenson know what he has, do you think?"

"He may and not care and so leave the chewink
To gather them for him—you know what he is.
He won't make the fact that they're rightfully his
An excuse for keeping us other folk out."

"I wonder you didn't see Loren about."

"The best of it was that I did. Do you know,
I was just getting through what the field had to show
And over the wall and into the road,
When who should come by, with a democrat-load
Of all the young chattering Lorens alive,
But Loren, the fatherly, out for a drive."

"He saw you, then? What did he do? Did he frown?"

"He just kept nodding his head up and down.
You know how politely he always goes by.
But he thought a big thought—I could tell by his eye—
Which being expressed, might be this in effect:
'I have left those there berries, I shrewdly suspect,
To ripen too long. I am greatly to blame.' "

"He's a thriftier person than some I could name."

"He seems to be thrifty; and hasn't he need,
With the mouths of all those young Lorens to feed?
He has brought them all up on wild berries, they say,
Like birds. They store a great many away.
They eat them the year round, and those they don't eat
They sell in the store and buy shoes for their feet."

"Who cares what they say? It's a nice way to live,
Just taking what Nature is willing to give,
Not forcing her hand with harrow and plow."

"I wish you had seen his perpetual bow—
And the air of the youngsters! Not one of them turned,
And they looked so solemn—absurdly concerned."

"I wish I knew half what the flock of them know
Of where all the berries and other things grow,
Cranberries in bogs and raspberries on top
Of the boulder-strewn mountain, and when they will
     crop.
I met them one day and each had a flower
Stuck into his berries as fresh as a shower;
Some strange kind—they told me it hadn't a name."

"I've told you how once not long after we came,
I almost provoked poor Loren to mirth
By going to him of all people on earth
To ask if he knew any fruit to be had
For the picking. The rascal, he said he'd be glad
To tell if he knew. But the year had been bad.
There *had* been some berries—but those were all gone.
He didn't say where they had been. He went on:
'I'm sure—I'm sure'—as polite as could be.
He spoke to his wife in the door, 'Let me see,
Mame, *we* don't know any good berrying place?'
It was all he could do to keep a straight face.

"If he thinks all the fruit that grows wild is for him,
He'll find he's mistaken. See here, for a whim,
We'll pick in the Mortensons' pasture this year.
We'll go in the morning, that is, if it's clear,
And the sun shines out warm: the vines must be wet.
It's so long since I picked I almost forget
How we used to pick berries: we took one look round,
Then sank out of sight like trolls underground,
And saw nothing more of each other, or heard,
Unless when you said I was keeping a bird

Away from its nest, and I said it was you.
'Well, one of us is.' For complaining it flew
Around and around us. And then for a while
We picked, till I feared you had wandered a mile,
And I thought I had lost you. I lifted a shout
Too loud for the distance you were, it turned out,
For when you made answer, your voice was as low
As talking—you stood up beside me, you know."

"We sha'n't have the place to ourselves to enjoy—
Not likely, when all the young Lorens deploy.
They'll be there tomorrow, or even tonight.
They won't be too friendly—they may be polite—
To people they look on as having no right
To pick where they're picking. But we won't complain.
You ought to have seen how it looked in the rain,
The fruit mixed with water in layers of leaves,
Like two kinds of jewels, a vision for thieves."

A SERVANT TO SERVANTS

I didn't make you know how glad I was
To have you come and camp here on our land.
I promised myself to get down some day
And see the way you lived, but I don't know!
With a houseful of hungry men to feed
I guess you'd find. . . . It seems to me
I can't express my feelings any more
Than I can raise my voice or want to lift
My hand (oh, I can lift it when I have to).
Did ever you feel so? I hope you never.
It's got so I don't even know for sure
Whether I *am* glad, sorry, or anything.
There's nothing but a voice-like left inside
That seems to tell me how I ought to feel,
And would feel if I wasn't all gone wrong.
You take the lake. I look and look at it.
I see it's a fair, pretty sheet of water.
I stand and make myself repeat out loud
The advantages it has, so long and narrow,
Like a deep piece of some old running river
Cut short off at both ends. It lies five miles
Straightaway through the mountain notch
From the sink window where I wash the plates,
And all our storms come up toward the house,
Drawing the slow waves whiter and whiter and whiter.
It took my mind off doughnuts and soda biscuit
To step outdoors and take the water dazzle
A sunny morning, or take the rising wind
About my face and body and through my wrapper,
When a storm threatened from the Dragon's Den,
And a cold chill shivered across the lake.
I see it's a fair, pretty sheet of water,

Our Willoughby! How did you hear of it?
I expect, though, everyone's heard of it.
In a book about ferns? Listen to that!
You let things more like feathers regulate
Your going and coming. And you like it here?
I can see how you might. But I don't know!
It would be different if more people came,
For then there would be business. As it is,
The cottages Len built, sometimes we rent them,
Sometimes we don't. We've a good piece of shore
That ought to be worth something, and may yet.
But I don't count on it as much as Len.
He looks on the bright side of everything,
Including me. He thinks I'll be all right
With doctoring. But it's not medicine—
Lowe is the only doctor's dared to say so—
It's rest I want—there, I have said it out—
From cooking meals for hungry hired men
And washing dishes after them—from doing
Things over and over that just won't stay done.
By good rights I ought not to have so much
Put on me, but there seems no other way.
Len says one steady pull more ought to do it.
He says the best way out is always through.
And I agree to that, or in so far
As that I can see no way out but through—
Leastways for me—and then they'll be convinced.
It's not that Len don't want the best for me.
It was his plan our moving over in
Beside the lake from where that day I showed you
We used to live—ten miles from anywhere.
We didn't change without some sacrifice,
But Len went at it to make up the loss.
His work's a man's, of course, from sun to sun,
But he works when he works as hard as I do—
Though there's small profit in comparisons.
(Women and men will make them all the same.)

But work ain't all. Len undertakes too much.
He's into everything in town. This year
It's highways, and he's got too many men
Around him to look after that make waste.
They take advantage of him shamefully,
And proud, too, of themselves for doing so.
We have four here to board, great good-for-nothings,
Sprawling about the kitchen with their talk
While I fry their bacon. Much they care!
No more put out in what they do or say
Than if I wasn't in the room at all.
Coming and going all the time, they are:
I don't learn what their names are, let alone
Their characters, or whether they are safe
To have inside the house with doors unlocked.
I'm not afraid of them, though, if they're not
Afraid of me. There's two can play at that.
I have my fancies: it runs in the family.
My father's brother wasn't right. They kept him
Locked up for years back there at the old farm.
I've been away once—yes, I've been away.
The State Asylum. I was prejudiced;
I wouldn't have sent anyone of mine there;
You know the old idea—the only asylum
Was the poorhouse, and those who could afford,
Rather than send their folks to such a place,
Kept them at home; and it does seem more human.
But it's not so: the place is the asylum.
There they have every means proper to do with,
And you aren't darkening other people's lives—
Worse than no good to them, and they no good
To you in your condition; you can't know
Affection or the want of it in that state.
I've heard too much of the old-fashioned way.
My father's brother, he went mad quite young.
Some thought he had been bitten by a dog,

Because his violence took on the form
Of carrying his pillow in his teeth;
But it's more likely he was crossed in love,
Or so the story goes. It was some girl.
Anyway all he talked about was love.
They soon saw he would do someone a mischief
If he wa'n't kept strict watch of, and it ended
In father's building him a sort of cage,
Or room within a room, of hickory poles,
Like stanchions in the barn, from floor to ceiling,—
A narrow passage all the way around.
Anything they put in for furniture
He'd tear to pieces, even a bed to lie on.
So they made the place comfortable with straw,
Like a beast's stall, to ease their consciences.
Of course they had to feed him without dishes.
They tried to keep him clothed, but he paraded
With his clothes on his arm—all of his clothes.
Cruel—it sounds. I 'spose they did the best
They knew. And just when he was at the height,
Father and mother married, and mother came,
A bride, to help take care of such a creature,
And accommodate her young life to his.
That was what marrying father meant to her.
She had to lie and hear love things made dreadful
By his shouts in the night. He'd shout and shout
Until the strength was shouted out of him,
And his voice died down slowly from exhaustion.
He'd pull his bars apart like bow and bowstring,
And let them go and make them twang until
His hands had worn them smooth as any oxbow.
And then he'd crow as if he thought that child's play—
The only fun he had. I've heard them say, though,
They found a way to put a stop to it.
He was before my time—I never saw him;
But the pen stayed exactly as it was

There in the upper chamber in the ell,
A sort of catchall full of attic clutter.
I often think of the smooth hickory bars.
It got so I would say—you know, half fooling—
"It's time I took my turn upstairs in jail"—
Just as you will till it becomes a habit.
No wonder I was glad to get away.
Mind you, I waited till Len said the word.
I didn't want the blame if things went wrong.
I was glad though, no end, when we moved out,
And I looked to be happy, and I was,
As I said, for a while—but I don't know!
Somehow the change wore out like a prescription.
And there's more to it than just window-views
And living by a lake. I'm past such help—
Unless Len took the notion, which he won't,
And I won't ask him—it's not sure enough.
I 'spose I've got to go the road I'm going:
Other folks have to, and why shouldn't I?
I almost think if I could do like you,
Drop everything and live out on the ground—
But it might be, come night, I shouldn't like it,
Or a long rain. I should soon get enough,
And be glad of a good roof overhead.
I've lain awake thinking of you, I'll warrant,
More than you have yourself, some of these nights.
The wonder was the tents weren't snatched away
From over you as you lay in your beds.
I haven't courage for a risk like that.
Bless you, of course, you're keeping me from work,
But the thing of it is, I need to *be* kept.
There's work enough to do—there's always that;
But behind's behind. The worst that you can do
Is set me back a little more behind.
I sha'n't catch up in this world, anyway.
I'd *rather* you'd not go unless you must.

AFTER APPLE-PICKING

My long two-pointed ladder's sticking through
    a tree
Toward heaven still,
And there's a barrel that I didn't fill
Beside it, and there may be two or three
Apples I didn't pick upon some bough.
But I am done with apple-picking now.
Essence of winter sleep is on the night,
The scent of apples: I am drowsing off.
I cannot rub the strangeness from my sight
I got from looking through a pane of glass
I skimmed this morning from the drinking trough
And held against the world of hoary grass.
It melted, and I let it fall and break.
But I was well
Upon my way to sleep before it fell,
And I could tell
What form my dreaming was about to take.
Magnified apples appear and disappear,
Stem end and blossom end,
And every fleck of russet showing clear.
My instep arch not only keeps the ache,
It keeps the pressure of a ladder-round.
I feel the ladder sway as the boughs bend.
And I keep hearing from the cellar bin
The rumbling sound
Of load on load of apples coming in.
For I have had too much
Of apple-picking: I am overtired
Of the great harvest I myself desired.
There were ten thousand thousand fruit to touch,
Cherish in hand, lift down, and not let fall.

For all
That struck the earth,
No matter if not bruised or spiked with stubble,
Went surely to the cider-apple heap
As of no worth.
One can see what will trouble
This sleep of mine, whatever sleep it is.
Were he not gone,
The woodchuck could say whether it's like his
Long sleep, as I describe its coming on,
Or just some human sleep.

THE CODE

There were three in the meadow by the brook
Gathering up windrows, piling cocks of hay,
With an eye always lifted toward the west
Where an irregular sun-bordered cloud
Darkly advanced with a perpetual dagger
Flickering across its bosom. Suddenly
One helper, thrusting pitchfork in the ground,
Marched himself off the field and home. One stayed.
The town-bred farmer failed to understand.

"What is there wrong?"

                              "Something you just now said."

"What did I say?"

                              "About our taking pains."

"To cock the hay?—because it's going to shower?
I said that more than half an hour ago.
I said it to myself as much as you."

"You didn't know. But James is one big fool.
He thought you meant to find fault with his work.
That's what the average farmer would have meant.
James would take time, of course, to chew it over
Before he acted: he's just got round to act."

"He is a fool if that's the way he takes me."

"Don't let it bother you. You've found out something.
The hand that knows his business won't be told

To do work better or faster—those two things.
I'm as particular as anyone:
Most likely I'd have served you just the same.
But I know you don't understand our ways.
You were just talking what was in your mind,
What was in all our minds, and you weren't hinting.
Tell you a story of what happened once:
I was up here in Salem at a man's
Named Sanders with a gang of four or five
Doing the haying. No one liked the boss.
He was one of the kind sports call a spider,
All wiry arms and legs that spread out wavy
From a humped body nigh as big's a biscuit.
But work! that man could work, especially
If by so doing he could get more work
Out of his hired help. I'm not denying
He was hard on himself. I couldn't find
That he kept any hours—not for himself.
Daylight and lantern-light were one to him:
I've heard him pounding in the barn all night.
But what he liked was someone to encourage.
Them that he couldn't lead he'd get behind
And drive, the way you can, you know, in mowing—
Keep at their heels and threaten to mow their legs off.
I'd seen about enough of his bulling tricks
(We call that bulling). I'd been watching him.
So when he paired off with me in the hayfield
To load the load, thinks I, Look out for trouble.
I built the load and topped it off; old Sanders
Combed it down with a rake and says, 'O. K.'
Everything went well till we reached the barn
With a big catch to empty in a bay.
You understand that meant the easy job
For the man up on top of throwing *down*
The hay and rolling it off wholesale,
Where on a mow it would have been slow lifting.
You wouldn't think a fellow'd need much urging

Under these circumstances, would you now?
But the old fool seizes his fork in both hands,
And looking up bewhiskered out of the pit,
Shouts like an army captain, 'Let her come!'
Thinks I, D'ye mean it? 'What was that you said?'
I asked out loud, so's there'd be no mistake,
'Did you say, Let her come?' 'Yes, let her come.'
He said it over, but he said it softer.
Never you say a thing like that to a man,
Not if he values what he is. God, I'd as soon
Murdered him as left out his middle name.
I'd built the load and knew right where to find it.
Two or three forkfuls I picked lightly round for
Like meditating, and then I just dug in
And dumped the rackful on him in ten lots.
I looked over the side once in the dust
And caught sight of him treading-water-like,
Keeping his head above. 'Damn ye,' I says,
'That gets ye!' He squeaked like a squeezed rat.
That was the last I saw or heard of him.
I cleaned the rack and drove out to cool off.
As I sat mopping hayseed from my neck,
And sort of waiting to be asked about it,
One of the boys sings out, 'Where's the old man?'
'I left him in the barn under the hay.
If ye want him, ye can go and dig him out.'
They realized from the way I swobbed my neck
More than was needed something must be up.
They headed for the barn; I stayed where I was.
They told me afterward. First they forked hay,
A lot of it, out into the barn floor.
Nothing! They listened for him. Not a rustle.
I guess they thought I'd spiked him in the temple
Before I buried him, or I couldn't have managed.
They excavated more. 'Go keep his wife
Out of the barn.' Someone looked in a window,
And curse me if he wasn't in the kitchen

Slumped way down in a chair, with both his feet
Stuck in the oven, the hottest day that summer.
He looked so clean disgusted from behind
There was no one that dared to stir him up,
Or let him know that he was being looked at.
Apparently I hadn't buried him
(I may have knocked him down); but my just trying
To bury him had hurt his dignity.
He had gone to the house so's not to meet me.
He kept away from us all afternoon.
We tended to his hay. We saw him out
After a while picking peas in his garden:
He couldn't keep away from doing something."

"Weren't you relieved to find he wasn't dead?"
"No! and yet I don't know—it's hard to say.
I went about to kill him fair enough."

"You took an awkward way. Did he discharge you?"

"Discharge me? No! He knew I did just right."

THE GENERATIONS OF MEN

A governor it was proclaimed this time,
When all who would come seeking in New Hampshire
Ancestral memories might come together.
And those of the name Stark gathered in Bow,
A rock-strewn town where farming has fallen off,
And sprout-lands flourish where the axe has gone.
Someone had literally run to earth
In an old cellar hole in a byroad
The origin of all the family there.
Thence they were sprung, so numerous a tribe
That now not all the houses left in town
Made shift to shelter them without the help
Of here and there a tent in grove and orchard.
They were at Bow, but that was not enough:
Nothing would do but they must fix a day
To stand together on the crater's verge
That turned them on the world, and try to fathom
The past and get some strangeness out of it.
But rain spoiled all. The day began uncertain,
With clouds low trailing and moments of rain that misted.
The young folk held some hope out to each other
Till well toward noon when the storm settled down
With a swish in the grass. "What if the others
Are there," they said. "It isn't going to rain."
Only one from a farm not far away
Strolled thither, not expecting he would find
Anyone else, but out of idleness.
One, and one other, yes, for there were two.
The second round the curving hillside road
Was a girl; and she halted some way off
To reconnoiter, and then made up her mind

—129—

At least to pass by and see who he was,
And perhaps hear some word about the weather.
This was some Stark she didn't know. He nodded.
"No fête today," he said.

                         "It looks that way."
She swept the heavens, turning on her heel.
"I only idled down."

                "I idled down."

Provision there had been for just such meeting
Of stranger cousins, in a family tree
Drawn on a sort of passport with the branch
Of the one bearing it done in detail—
Some zealous one's laborious device.
She made a sudden movement toward her bodice,
As one who clasps her heart. They laughed together.
"Stark?" he inquired. "No matter for the proof."

"Yes, Stark. And you?"

                "I'm Stark." He drew his passport.

"You know we might not be and still be cousins:
The town is full of Chases, Lowes, and Baileys,
All claiming some priority in Starkness.
My mother was a Lane, yet might have married
Anyone upon earth and still her children
Would have been Starks, and doubtless here today."

"You riddle with your genealogy
Like a Viola. I don't follow you."

"I only mean my mother was a Stark
Several times over, and by marrying father
No more than brought us back into the name."

"One ought not to be thrown into confusion
By a plain statement of relationship,
But I own what you say makes my head spin.
You take my card—you seem so good at such things—
And see if you can reckon our cousinship.
Why not take seats here on the cellar wall
And dangle feet among the raspberry vines?"

"Under the shelter of the family tree."

"Just so—that ought to be enough protection."

"Not from the rain. I think it's going to rain."

"It's raining."

       "No, it's misting; let's be fair.
Does the rain seem to you to cool the eyes?"

The situation was like this: the road
Bowed outward on the mountain halfway up,
And disappeared and ended not far off.
No one went home that way. The only house
Beyond where they were was a shattered seedpod.
And below roared a brook hidden in trees,
The sound of which was silence for the place.
This he sat listening to till she gave judgment.

"On father's side, it seems, we're—let me see——"

"Don't be too technical.—You have three cards."

"Four cards, one yours, three mine, one for each branch
Of the Stark family I'm a member of."

"D'you know a person so related to herself
Is supposed to be mad."

                                    "I may be mad."

"You look so, sitting out here in the rain
Studying genealogy with me
You never saw before. What will we come to
With all this pride of ancestry, we Yankees?
I think we're all mad. Tell me why we're here
Drawn into town about this cellar hole
Like wild geese on a lake before a storm?
What do we see in such a hole, I wonder."

"The Indians had a myth of Chicamoztoc,
Which means The Seven Caves that We Came out of.
This is the pit from which we Starks were digged."

"You must be learned. That's what you see in it?"

"And what do you see?"

                          "Yes, what *do* I see?
First let me look. I see raspberry vines——"

"Oh, if you're going to use your eyes, just hear
What *I* see. It's a little, little boy,
As pale and dim as a match flame in the sun;
He's groping in the cellar after jam,
He thinks it's dark and it's flooded with daylight."

"He's nothing. Listen. When I lean like this
I can make out old Grandsir Stark distinctly,—
With his pipe in his mouth and his brown jug—
Bless you, it isn't Grandsir Stark, it's Granny,
But the pipe's there and smoking and the jug.

She's after cider, the old girl, she's thirsty;
Here's hoping she gets her drink and gets out safely."

"Tell me about her. Does she look like me?"

"She should, shouldn't she, you're so many times
Over descended from her. I believe
She does look like you. Stay the way you are.
The nose is just the same, and so's the chin—
Making allowance, making due allowance."

"You poor, dear, great, great, great, great Granny!"

"See that you get her greatness right. Don't stint her."

"Yes, it's important, though you think it isn't.
I won't be teased. But see how wet I am."

"Yes, you must go; we can't stay here for ever.
But wait until I give you a hand up.
A bead of silver water more or less
Strung on your hair won't hurt your summer looks.
I wanted to try something with the noise
That the brook raises in the empty valley.
We have seen visions—now consult the voices.
Something I must have learned riding in trains
When I was young. I used the roar
To set the voices speaking out of it,
Speaking or singing, and the band-music playing.
Perhaps you have the art of what I mean.
I've never listened in among the sounds
That a brook makes in such a wild descent.
It ought to give a purer oracle."

"It's as you throw a picture on a screen:
The meaning of it all is out of you;
The voices give you what you wish to hear."

"Strangely, it's anything they wish to give."

"Then I don't know. It must be strange enough.
I wonder if it's not your make-believe.
What do you think you're like to hear today?"

"From the sense of our having been together—
But why take time for what I'm like to hear?
I'll tell you what the voices really say.
You will do very well right where you are
A little longer. I mustn't feel too hurried,
Or I can't give myself to hear the voices."

"Is this some trance you are withdrawing into?"

"You must be very still; you mustn't talk."

"I'll hardly breathe."

                    "The voices seem to say——"

"I'm waiting."

                    "Don't! The voices seem to say:
Call her Nausicaa, the unafraid
Of an acquaintance made adventurously."

"I let you say that—on consideration."

"I don't see very well how you can help it.
You want the truth. I speak but by the voices.
You see they know I haven't had your name,
Though what a name should matter between us—"
"I shall suspect——"

                    "Be good. The voices say:
Call her Nausicaa, and take a timber
That you shall find lies in the cellar charred

— 134 —

Among the raspberries, and hew and shape it
For a doorsill or other corner piece
In a new cottage on the ancient spot.
The life is not yet all gone out of it.
And come and make your summer dwelling here,
And perhaps she will come, still unafraid,
And sit before you in the open door
With flowers in her lap until they fade,
But not come in across the sacred sill—''

"I wonder where your oracle is tending.
You can see that there's something wrong with it,
Or it would speak in dialect. Whose voice
Does it purport to speak in? Not old Grandsir's
Nor Granny's, surely. Call up one of them.
They have best right to be heard in this place."

"You seem so partial to our great-grandmother
(Nine times removed. Correct me if I err.)
You will be likely to regard as sacred
Anything she may say. But let me warn you,
Folks in her day were given to plain speaking.
You think you'd best tempt her at such a time?"

"It rests with us always to cut her off."

"Well then, it's Granny speaking: 'I dunnow!
Mebbe I'm wrong to take it as I do.
There ain't no names quite like the old ones though,
Nor never will be to my way of thinking.
One mustn't bear too hard on the newcomers,
But there's a dite too many of them for comfort.
I should feel easier if I could see
More of the salt wherewith they're to be salted.
Son, you do as you're told! You take the timber—
It's as sound as the day when it was cut—
And begin over——' There, she'd better stop.

You can see what is troubling Granny, though.
But don't you think we sometimes make too much
Of the old stock? What counts is the ideals,
And those will bear some keeping still about."

"I can see we are going to be good friends."

"I like your 'going to be.' You said just now
It's going to rain."

                    "I know, and it was raining.
I let you say all that. But I must go now."

"You let me say it? on consideration?
How shall we say good-bye in such a case?"

"How shall we?"

            "Will you leave the way to me?"

"No, I don't trust your eyes. You've said
    enough.
Now give me your hand up.—Pick me that flower."

"Where shall we meet again?"

                    "Nowhere but here
Once more before we meet elsewhere."

                        "In rain?"
"It ought to be in rain. Sometime in rain.
In rain tomorrow, shall we, if it rains?
But if we must, in sunshine." So she went.

THE HOUSEKEEPER

I let myself in at the kitchen door.

"It's you," *she said.* "I can't get up. Forgive me
Not answering your knock. I can no more
Let people in than I can keep them out.
I'm getting too old for my size, I tell them.
My fingers are about all I've the use of
So's to take any comfort. I can sew:
I help out with this beadwork what I can."

"That's a smart pair of pumps you're beading there.
Who are they for?"

               "You mean?—oh, for some miss.
I can't keep track of other people's daughters.
Lord, if I were to dream of everyone
Whose shoes I primped to dance in!"

                       "And where's John?"

"Haven't you seen him? Strange what set you off
To come to his house when he's gone to yours.
You can't have passed each other. I know what:
He must have changed his mind and gone to
    Garlands.
He won't be long in that case. You can wait.
Though what good you can be, or anyone—
It's gone so far. You've heard? Estelle's run off."

"Yes, what's it all about? When did she go?"

"Two weeks since."

           "She's in earnest, it appears."

"I'm sure she won't come back. She's hiding some-
    where.
I don't know where myself. John thinks I do.
He thinks I only have to say the word,
And she'll come back. But, bless you, I'm her mother—
I can't talk to her, and, Lord, if I could!"

"It will go hard with John. What will he do?
He can't find anyone to take her place."

"Oh, if you ask me that, what *will* he do?
He gets some sort of bakeshop meals together,
With me to sit and tell him everything,
What's wanted and how much and where it is.
But when I'm gone—of course I can't stay here:
Estelle's to take me when she's settled down.
He and I only hinder one another.
I tell them they can't get me through the door, though:
I've been built in here like a big church organ.
We've been here fifteen years."

                              "That's a long time
To live together and then pull apart.
How do you see him living when you're gone?
Two of you out will leave an empty house."

"I don't just see him living many years,
Left here with nothing but the furniture.
I hate to think of the old place when we're gone,
With the brook going by below the yard,
And no one here but hens blowing about.
If he could sell the place, but then, he can't:
No one will ever live on it again.
It's too run down. This is the last of it.
What I think he will do, is let things smash.
He'll sort of swear the time away. He's awful!
I never saw a man let family troubles
Make so much difference in his man's affairs.

He's just dropped everything. He's like a child.
I blame his being brought up by his mother.
He's got hay down that's been rained on three times.
He hoed a little yesterday for me:
I thought the growing things would do him good.
Something went wrong. I saw him throw the hoe
Sky-high with both hands. I can see it now—
Come here—I'll show you—in that apple tree.
That's no way for a man to do at his age:
He's fifty-five, you know, if he's a day."

"Aren't you afraid of him? What's that gun for?"

"Oh, that's been there for hawks since chicken-time.
John Hall touch me! Not if he knows his friends.
I'll say that for him, John's no threatener
Like some men folk. No one's afraid of him;
All is, he's made up his mind not to stand
What he has got to stand."

                          "Where is Estelle?
Couldn't one talk to her? What does she say?
You say you don't know where she is."

                          "Nor want to!
She thinks if it was bad to live with him,
It must be right to leave him."

                          "Which is wrong!"

"Yes, but he should have married her."

                          "I know."

"The strain's been too much for her all these years:
I can't explain it any other way.
It's different with a man, at least with John:

He knows he's kinder than the run of men.
Better than married ought to be as good
As married—that's what he has always said.
I know the way he's felt—but all the same!"

"I wonder why he doesn't marry her
And end it."

      "Too late now: she wouldn't have him.
He's given her time to think of something else.
That's his mistake. The dear knows my interest
Has been to keep the thing from breaking up.
This is a good home: I don't ask for better.
But when I've said, 'Why shouldn't they be married,'
He'd say, 'Why should they?' no more words than that."

"And after all why should they? John's been fair
I take it. What was his was always hers.
There was no quarrel about property."

"Reason enough, there was no property.
A friend or two as good as own the farm,
Such as it is. It isn't worth the mortgage."

"I mean Estelle has always held the purse."

"The rights of that are harder to get at.
I guess Estelle and I have filled the purse.
'Twas we let him have money, not he us.
John's a bad farmer. I'm not blaming him.
Take it year in, year out, he doesn't make much.
We came here for a home for me, you know,
Estelle to do the housework for the board
Of both of us. But look how it turns out:
She seems to have the housework, and besides
Half of the outdoor work, though as for that,
He'd say she does it more because she likes it.

You see our pretty things are all outdoors.
Our hens and cows and pigs are always better
Than folks like us have any business with.
Farmers around twice as well off as we
Haven't as good. They don't go with the farm.
One thing you can't help liking about John,
He's fond of nice things—too fond, some would say.
But Estelle don't complain: she's like him there.
She wants our hens to be the best there are.
You never saw this room before a show,
Full of lank, shivery, half-drowned birds
In separate coops, having their plumage done.
The smell of the wet feathers in the heat!
You spoke of John's not being safe to stay with.
You don't know what a gentle lot we are:
We wouldn't hurt a hen! You ought to see us
Moving a flock of hens from place to place.
We're not allowed to take them upside down,
All we can hold together by the legs.
Two at a time's the rule, one on each arm,
No matter how far and how many times
We have to go."

                    "You mean that's John's idea."

"And we live up to it; or I don't know
What childishness he wouldn't give way to.
He manages to keep the upper hand
On his own farm. He's boss. But as to hens:
We fence our flowers in and the hens range.
Nothing's too good for them. We say it pays.
John likes to tell the offers he has had,
Twenty for this cock, twenty-five for that.
He never takes the money. If they're worth
That much to sell, they're worth as much to keep.
Bless you, it's all expense, though. Reach me down

—141—

The little tin box on the cupboard shelf,
The upper shelf, the tin box. That's the one.
I'll show you. Here you are."

"What's this?"

"A bill—
For fifty dollars for one Langshang cock—
Receipted. And the cock is in the yard."

"Not in a glass case, then?"

"He'd need a tall one:
He can eat off a barrel from the ground.
He's been in a glass case, as you may say,
The Crystal Palace, London. He's imported.
John bought him, and we paid the bill with beads—
Wampum, I call it. Mind, we don't complain.
But you see, don't you, we take care of him."

"And like it, too. It makes it all the worse."

"It seems as if. And that's not all: he's helpless
In ways that I can hardly tell you of.
Sometimes he gets possessed to keep accounts
To see where all the money goes so fast.
You know how men will be ridiculous.
But it's just fun the way he gets bedeviled—
If he's untidy now, what will he be——?"

"It makes it all the worse. You must be blind."

"Estelle's the one. You needn't talk to me."

"Can't you and I get to the root of it?
What's the real trouble? What will satisfy her?"

"It's as I say: she's turned from him, that's all."

"But why, when she's well off? Is it the neighbors,
Being cut off from friends?"

                              "We have our friends.
That isn't it. Folks aren't afraid of us."

"She's let it worry her. You stood the strain,
And you're her mother."

                              "But I didn't always.
I didn't relish it along at first.
But I got wonted to it. And besides—
John said I was too old to have grandchildren.
But what's the use of talking when it's done?
She won't come back—it's worse than that—she can't."

"Why do you speak like that? What do you know?
What do you mean?—she's done harm to herself?"

"I mean she's married—married someone else."

"Oho, oho!"

          "You don't believe me."

                              "Yes, I do,
Only too well. I knew there must be something!
So that was what was back. She's bad, that's all!"

"Bad to get married when she had the chance?"

"Nonsense! See what's she done! But who, who——"

"Who'd marry her straight out of such a mess?
Say it right out—no matter for her mother.

—143—

The man was found. I'd better name no names.
John himself won't imagine who he is."

"Then it's all up. I think I'll get away.
You'll be expecting John. I pity Estelle;
I suppose she deserves some pity, too.
You ought to have the kitchen to yourself
To break it to him. You may have the job."

"You needn't think you're going to get away.
John's almost here. I've had my eye on someone
Coming down Ryan's Hill. I thought 'twas him.
Here he is now. This box! Put it away.
And this bill."

                    "What's the hurry? He'll unhitch."

"No, he won't, either. He'll just drop the reins
And turn Doll out to pasture, rig and all.
She won't get far before the wheels hang up
On something—there's no harm. See, there he is!
My, but he looks as if he must have heard!"

John threw the door wide but he didn't enter.
"How are you, neighbor? Just the man I'm after.
Isn't it Hell," *he said.* "I want to know.
Come out here if you want to hear me talk.
I'll talk to you, old woman, afterward.
I've got some news that maybe isn't news.
What are they trying to do to me, these two?"

"Do go along with him and stop his shouting."
She raised her voice against the closing door:
"Who wants to hear your news, you—dreadful fool?"

THE FEAR

A lantern light from deeper in the barn
Shone on a man and woman in the door
And threw their lurching shadows on a house
Near by, all dark in every glossy window.
A horse's hoof pawed once the hollow floor,
And the back of the gig they stood beside
Moved in a little. The man grasped a wheel,
The woman spoke out sharply, "Whoa, stand still!"
"I saw it just as plain as a white plate,"
She said, "as the light on the dashboard ran
Along the bushes at the roadside—a man's face.
You *must* have seen it too."

                                        "I didn't see it.
Are you sure——"

                    "Yes, I'm sure!"

                                "—it was a face?"

"Joel, I'll have to look. I can't go in,
I can't, and leave a thing like that unsettled.
Doors locked and curtains drawn will make no
        difference.
I always have felt strange when we came home
To the dark house after so long an absence,
And the key rattled loudly into place
Seemed to warn someone to be getting out
At one door as we entered at another.
What if I'm right, and someone all the time—
Don't hold my arm!"

                    "I say it's someone passing."

"You speak as if this were a traveled road.
You forget where we are. What is beyond
That he'd be going to or coming from
At such an hour of night, and on foot too.
What was he standing still for in the bushes?"

"It's not so very late—it's only dark.
There's more in it than you're inclined to say.
Did he look like——?"

                              "He looked like anyone.
I'll never rest tonight unless I know.
Give me the lantern."

                         "You don't want the lantern."

She pushed past him and got it for herself.

"You're not to come," she said. "This is my business.
If the time's come to face it, I'm the one
To put it the right way. He'd never dare—
Listen! He kicked a stone. Hear that, hear that!
He's coming towards us. Joel, *go* in—please.
Hark!—I don't hear him now. But please go in."

"In the first place you can't make me believe it's——"

"It is—or someone else he's sent to watch.
And now's the time to have it out with him
While we know definitely where he is.
Let him get off and he'll be everywhere
Around us, looking out of trees and bushes
Till I sha'n't dare to set a foot outdoors.
And I can't stand it. Joel, let me go!"

"But it's nonsense to think he'd care enough."

"You mean you couldn't understand his caring.
Oh, but you see he hadn't had enough—
Joel, I won't—I won't—I promise you.
We mustn't say hard things. You mustn't either."

"I'll be the one, if anybody goes!
But you give him the advantage with this light.
What couldn't he do to us standing here!
And if to see was what he wanted, why
He has seen all there was to see and gone."

He appeared to forget to keep his hold,
But advanced with her as she crossed the grass.

"What do you want?" she cried to all the dark.
She stretched up tall to overlook the light
That hung in both hands hot against her skirt.

"There's no one; so you're wrong," he said.

                                   "There is.—
What do you want?" she cried, and then herself
Was startled when an answer really came.

"Nothing." It came from well along the road.

She reached a hand to Joel for support:
The smell of scorching woollen made her faint.

"What are you doing round this house at night?"

"Nothing." A pause: there seemed no more to say.

And then the voice again: "You seem afraid.
I saw by the way you whipped up the horse.

I'll just come forward in the lantern light
And let you see."

                    "Yes, do.—Joel, go back!"

She stood her ground against the noisy steps
That came on, but her body rocked a little.

"You see," the voice said.

                    "Oh." She looked and looked.

"You don't see—I've a child here by the hand."

"What's a child doing at this time of night——?"

"Out walking. Every child should have the memory
Of at least one long-after-bedtime walk.
What, son?"

            "Then I should think you'd try to find
Somewhere to walk——"

            "The highway as it happens—
We're stopping for the fortnight down at Dean's."

"But if that's all—Joel—you realize—
You won't think anything. You understand?
You understand that we have to be careful.
This is a very, very lonely place.
Joel!" She spoke as if she couldn't turn.
The swinging lantern lengthened to the ground,
It touched, it struck it, clattered and went out.

THE SELF-SEEKER

"Willis, I didn't want you here today:
The lawyer's coming for the company.
I'm going to sell my soul, or, rather, feet.
Five hundred dollars for the pair, you know."

"With you the feet have nearly been the soul;
And if you're going to sell them to the devil,
I want to see you do it. When's he coming?"

"I half suspect you knew, and came on purpose
To try to help me drive a better bargain."

"Well, if it's true! Yours are no common feet.
The lawyer don't know what it is he's buying:
So many miles you might have walked you won't walk.
You haven't run your forty orchids down.
What does he think?—How *are* the blessed feet?
The doctor's sure you're going to walk again?"

"He thinks I'll hobble. It's both legs and feet."

"They must be terrible—I mean to look at."

"I haven't dared to look at them uncovered.
Through the bed blankets I remind myself
Of a starfish laid out with rigid points."

"The wonder is it hadn't been your head."

"It's hard to tell you how I managed it.
When I saw the shaft had me by the coat,

I didn't try too long to pull away,
Or fumble for my knife to cut away,
I just embraced the shaft and rode it out—
Till Weiss shut off the water in the wheel-pit.
That's how I think I didn't lose my head.
But my legs got their knocks against the ceiling."

"Awful. Why didn't they throw off the belt
Instead of going clear down in the wheel-pit?"

"They say some time was wasted on the belt—
Old streak of leather—doesn't love me much
Because I make him spit fire at my knuckles,
The way Ben Franklin used to make the kite-string.
That must be it. Some days he won't stay on.
That day a woman couldn't coax him off.
He's on his rounds now with his tail in his mouth
Snatched right and left across the silver pulleys.
Everything goes the same without me there.
You can hear the small buzz saws whine, the big saw
Caterwaul to the hills around the village
As they both bite the wood. It's all our music.
One ought as a good villager to like it.
No doubt it has a sort of prosperous sound,
And it's our life."

                              "Yes, when it's not our death."

"You make that sound as if it wasn't so
With everything. What we live by we die by.
I wonder where my lawyer is. His train's in.
I want this over with; I'm hot and tired."

"You're getting ready to do something foolish."

"Watch for him, will you, Will? You let him in.
I'd rather Mrs. Corbin didn't know;

I've boarded here so long, she thinks she owns me.
You're bad enough to manage without her."

"And I'm going to be worse instead of better.
You've got to tell me how far this is gone:
Have you agreed to any price?"

                                    "Five hundred.
Five hundred—five—five! One, two, three, four, five.
You needn't look at me."

                    "I don't believe you."

"I told you, Willis, when you first came in.
Don't you be hard on me. I have to take
What I can get. You see they have the feet,
Which gives them the advantage in the trade.
I can't get back the feet in any case."

"But your flowers, man, you're selling out your flowers."

"Yes, that's one way to put it—all the flowers
Of every kind everywhere in this region
For the next forty summers—call it forty.
But I'm not selling those, I'm giving them,
They never earned me so much as one cent:
Money can't pay me for the loss of them.
No, the five hundred was the sum they named
To pay the doctor's bill and tide me over.
It's that or fight, and I don't want to fight—
I just want to get settled in my life,
Such as it's going to be, and know the worst,
Or best—it may not be so bad. The firm
Promise me all the shooks I want to nail."

"But what about your flora of the valley?"

"You have me there. But that—you didn't think
That was worth money to me? Still I own
It goes against me not to finish it
For the friends it might bring me. By the way,
I had a letter from Burroughs—did I tell you?—
About my *Cyprepedium reginæ;*
He says it's not reported so far north.
There! there's the bell. He's rung. But you go down
And bring him up, and don't let Mrs. Corbin.—
Oh, well, we'll soon be through with it. I'm tired."

Willis brought up besides the Boston lawyer
A little barefoot girl who in the noise
Of heavy footsteps in the old frame house,
And baritone importance of the lawyer,
Stood for a while unnoticed with her hands
Shyly behind her.

                    "Well, and how is Mister——"
The lawyer was already in his satchel
As if for papers that might bear the name
He hadn't at command. "You must excuse me,
I dropped in at the mill and was detained."

"Looking round, I suppose," said Willis.

                                        "Yes,
Well, yes."

"Hear anything that might prove useful?"

The Broken One saw Anne. "Why, here is Anne.
What do you want, dear? Come, stand by the bed;
Tell me what is it?" Anne just wagged her dress
With both hands held behind her. "Guess," she said.

"Oh, guess which hand? My, my! Once on a time
I knew a lovely way to tell for certain

By looking in the ears. But I forget it.
Er, let me see. I think I'll take the right.
That's sure to be right even if it's wrong.
Come, hold it out. Don't change.—A Ram's Horn
    orchid!
A Ram's Horn! What would I have got, I wonder,
If I had chosen left. Hold out the left.
Another Ram's Horn! Where did you find those,
Under what beech tree, on what woodchuck's knoll?"

Anne looked at the large lawyer at her side,
And thought she wouldn't venture on so much.

"Were there no others?"

                        "There were four or five.
I knew you wouldn't let me pick them all."

"I wouldn't—so I wouldn't. You're the girl!
You see Anne has her lesson learned by heart."

"I wanted there should be some there next year."

"Of course you did. You left the rest for seed,
And for the backwoods woodchuck. You're the girl!
A Ram's Horn orchid seedpod for a woodchuck
Sounds something like. Better than farmer's beans
To a discriminating appetite,
Though the Ram's Horn is seldom to be had
In bushel lots—doesn't come on the market.
But, Anne, I'm troubled; have you told me all?
You're hiding something. That's as bad as lying.
You ask this lawyer man. And it's not safe
With a lawyer at hand to find you out.
Nothing is hidden from some people, Anne.
You don't tell me that where you found a Ram's Horn

You didn't find a Yellow Lady's Slipper.
What did I tell you? What? I'd blush, I would.
Don't you defend yourself. If it was there,
Where is it now, the Yellow Lady's Slipper?"

"Well, wait—it's common—it's too *common*."

                                      "Common?
The Purple Lady's Slipper's commoner."

"I didn't bring a Purple Lady's Slipper
To *You*—to you I mean—they're both too common."

The lawyer gave a laugh among his papers
As if with some idea that she had scored.

"I've broken Anne of gathering bouquets.
It's not fair to the child. It can't be helped though:
Pressed into service means pressed out of shape.
Somehow I'll make it right with her—she'll see.
She's going to do my scouting in the field,
Over stone walls and all along a wood
And by a river bank for water flowers,
The floating Heart, with small leaf like a heart,
And at the *sinus* under water a fist
Of little fingers all kept down but one,
And that thrust up to blossom in the sun
As if to say, 'You! You're the Heart's desire.'
Anne has a way with flowers to take the place
Of that she's lost: she goes down on one knee
And lifts their faces by the chin to hers
And says their names, and leaves them where they are."

The lawyer wore a watch the case of which
Was cunningly devised to make a noise
Like a small pistol when he snapped it shut
At such a time as this. He snapped it now.

"Well, Anne, go, dearie. Our affair will wait.
The lawyer man is thinking of his train.
He wants to give me lots and lots of money
Before he goes, because I hurt myself,
And it may take him I don't know how long.
But put our flowers in water first. Will, help her:
The pitcher's too full for her. There's no cup?
Just hook them on the inside of the pitcher.
Now run.—Get out your documents! You see
I have to keep on the good side of Anne.
I'm a great boy to think of number one.
And you can't blame me in the place I'm in.
Who will take care of my necessities
Unless I do?"

          "A pretty interlude,"
The lawyer said. "I'm sorry, but my train—
Luckily terms are all agreed upon.
You only have to sign your name. Right—there."

"You, Will, stop making faces. Come round here
Where you can't make them. What is it you want?
I'll put you out with Anne. Be good or go."

"You don't mean you will sing that thing unread?"

"Make yourself useful then, and read it for me.
Isn't it something I have seen before?"

"You'll find it is. Let your friend look at it."

"Yes, but all that takes time, and I'm as much
In haste to get it over with as you.
But read it, read it. That's right, draw the curtain:
Half the time I don't know what's troubling me.—
What do you say, Will? Don't you be a fool,

You! crumpling folkses legal documents.
Out with it if you've any real objection."

"Five hundred dollars!"

                    "What would you think right?"

"A thousand wouldn't be a cent too much;
You know it, Mr. Lawyer. The sin is
Accepting anything before he knows
Whether he's ever going to walk again.
It smells to me like a dishonest trick."

"I think—I think—from what I heard today—
And saw myself—he would be ill-advised——"

"What did you hear, for instance?" Willis said.

"Now the place where the accident occurred——"

The Broken One was twisted in his bed.
"This is between you two apparently.
Where I come in is what I want to know.
You stand up to it like a pair of cocks.
Go outdoors if you want to fight. Spare me.
When you come back, I'll have the papers signed.
Will pencil do? Then, please, your fountain pen.
One of you hold my head up from the pillow."

Willis flung off the bed. "I wash my hands—
I'm no match—no, and don't pretend to be——"

The lawyer gravely capped his fountain pen.
"You're doing the wise thing: you won't regret it.
We're very sorry for you."

Willis sneered:
"Who's *we?*—some stockholders in Boston?
I'll go outdoors, by gad, and won't come back."

"Willis, bring Anne back with you when you come.
Yes. Thanks for caring. Don't mind Will: he's savage.
He thinks you ought to pay me for my flowers.
You don't know what I mean about the flowers.
Don't stop to try to now. You'll miss your train.
Good-bye." He flung his arms around his face.

THE WOOD-PILE

Out walking in the frozen swamp one gray day
I paused and said, "I will turn back from here.
No, I will go on farther—and we shall see."
The hard snow held me, save where now and then
One foot went down. The view was all in lines
Straight up and down of tall slim trees
Too much alike to mark or name a place by
So as to say for certain I was here
Or somewhere else: I was just far from home.
A small bird flew before me. He was careful
To put a tree between us when he lighted,
And say no word to tell me who he was
Who was so foolish as to think what *he* thought.
He thought that I was after him for a feather—
The white one in his tail; like one who takes
Everything said as personal to himself.
One flight out sideways would have undeceived him.
And then there was a pile of wood for which
I forgot him and let his little fear
Carry him off the way I might have gone,
Without so much as wishing him good night.
He went behind it to make his last stand.
It was a cord of maple, cut and split
And piled—and measured, four by four by eight.
And not another like it could I see.
No runner tracks in this year's snow looped near it.
And it was older sure than this year's cutting,
Or even last year's or the year's before.
The wood was gray and the bark warping off it
And the pile somewhat sunken. Clematis
Had wound strings round and round it like a bundle.

What held it though on one side was a tree
Still growing, and on one a stake and prop,
These latter about to fall. I thought that only
Someone who lived in turning to fresh tasks
Could so forget his handiwork on which
He spent himself, the labor of his axe,
And leave it there far from a useful fireplace
To warm the frozen swamp as best it could
With the slow smokeless burning of decay.

GOOD HOURS

I had for my winter evening walk—
No one at all with whom to talk,
But I had the cottages in a row
Up to their shining eyes in snow.

And I thought I had the folk within:
I had the sound of a violin;
I had a glimpse through curtain laces
Of youthful forms and youthful faces.

I had such company outward bound.
I went till there were no cottages found.
I turned and repented, but coming back
I saw no window but that was black.

Over the snow my creaking feet
Disturbed the slumbering village street
Like profanation, by your leave,
At ten o'clock of a winter eve.

Mountain Interval

THE ROAD NOT TAKEN

Two roads diverged in a yellow wood,
And sorry I could not travel both
And be one traveler, long I stood
And looked down one as far as I could
To where it bent in the undergrowth;

Then took the other, as just as fair,
And having perhaps the better claim,
Because it was grassy and wanted wear;
Though as for that the passing there
Had worn them really about the same,

And both that morning equally lay
In leaves no step had trodden black.
Oh, I kept the first for another day!
Yet knowing how way leads on to way,
I doubted if I should ever come back.

I shall be telling this with a sigh
Somewhere ages and ages hence:
Two roads diverged in a wood, and I—
I took the one less traveled by,
And that has made all the difference.

CHRISTMAS TREES

(A Christmas Circular Letter)

The city had withdrawn into itself
And left at last the country to the country;
When between whirls of snow not come to lie
And whirls of foliage not yet laid, there drove
A stranger to our yard, who looked the city,
Yet did in country fashion in that there
He sat and waited till he drew us out
A-buttoning coats to ask him who he was.
He proved to be the city come again
To look for something it had left behind
And could not do without and keep its Christmas.
He asked if I would sell my Christmas trees;
My woods—the young fir balsams like a place
Where houses all are churches and have spires.
I hadn't thought of them as Christmas Trees.
I doubt if I was tempted for a moment
To sell them off their feet to go in cars
And leave the slope behind the house all bare,
Where the sun shines now no warmer than the moon.
I'd hate to have them know it if I was.
Yet more I'd hate to hold my trees except
As others hold theirs or refuse for them,
Beyond the time of profitable growth,
The trial by market everything must come to.
I dallied so much with the thought of selling.
Then whether from mistaken courtesy
And fear of seeming short of speech, or whether
From hope of hearing good of what was mine,
I said, "There aren't enough to be worth while."

"I could soon tell how many they would cut,
You let me look them over."

                      "You could look.
But don't expect I'm going to let you have them."
Pasture they spring in, some in clumps too close
That lop each other of boughs, but not a few
Quite solitary and having equal boughs
All round and round. The latter he nodded "Yes" to,
Or paused to say beneath some lovelier one,
With a buyer's moderation, "That would do."
I thought so too, but wasn't there to say so.
We climbed the pasture on the south, crossed over,
And came down on the north.

                      He said, "A thousand."

"A thousand Christmas trees!—at what apiece?"

He felt some need of softening that to me:
"A thousand trees would come to thirty dollars."

Then I was certain I had never meant
To let him have them. Never show surprise!
But thirty dollars seemed so small beside
The extent of pasture I should strip, three cents
(For that was all they figured out apiece)
Three cents so small beside the dollar friends
I should be writing to within the hour
Would pay in cities for good trees like those,
Regular vestry-trees whole Sunday Schools
Could hang enough on to pick off enough.

A thousand Christmas trees I didn't know I had!
Worth three cents more to give away than sell,
As may be shown by a simple calculation.
Too bad I couldn't lay one in a letter.
I can't help wishing I could send you one,
In wishing you here with a Merry Christmas.

AN OLD MAN'S WINTER NIGHT

All out of doors looked darkly in at him
Through the thin frost, almost in separate stars,
That gathers on the pane in empty rooms.
What kept his eyes from giving back the gaze
Was the lamp tilted near them in his hand.
What kept him from remembering what it was
That brought him to that creaking room was age.
He stood with barrels round him—at a loss.
And having scared the cellar under him
In clomping there, he scared it once again
In clomping off;—and scared the outer night,
Which has its sounds, familiar, like the roar
Of trees and crack of branches, common things,
But nothing so like beating on a box.
A light he was to no one but himself
Where now he sat, concerned with he knew what,
A quiet light, and then not even that.
He consigned to the moon, such as she was,
So late-arising, to the broken moon
As better than the sun in any case
For such a charge, his snow upon the roof,
His icicles along the wall to keep;
And slept. The log that shifted with a jolt
Once in the stove, disturbed him and he shifted,
And eased his heavy breathing, but still slept.
One aged man—one man—can't fill a house,
A farm, a countryside, or if he can,
It's thus he does it of a winter night.

A PATCH OF OLD SNOW

There's a patch of old snow in a corner
   That I should have guessed
Was a blow-away paper the rain
   Had brought to rest.

It is speckled with grime as if
   Small print overspread it,
The news of a day I've forgotten—
   If I ever read it.

IN THE HOME STRETCH

She stood against the kitchen sink, and looked
Over the sink out through a dusty window
At weeds the water from the sink made tall.
She wore her cape; her hat was in her hand.
Behind her was confusion in the room,
Of chairs turned upside down to sit like people
In other chairs, and something, come to look,
For every room a house has—parlor, bedroom,
And dining-room—thrown pell-mell in the kitchen.
And now and then a smudged, infernal face
Looked in a door behind her and addressed
Her back. She always answered without turning.

"Where will I put this walnut bureau, lady?"

"Put it on top of something that's on top
Of something else," she laughed. "Oh, put it where
You can tonight, and go. It's almost dark;
You must be getting started back to town."
Another blackened face thrust in and looked
And smiled, and when she did not turn, spoke gently,
"What are you seeing out the window, *lady?*"

"Never was I beladied so before.
Would evidence of having been called lady
More than so many times make me a lady
In common law, I wonder."

                              "But I ask,
What are you seeing out the window, lady?"

"What I'll be seeing more of in the years
To come as here I stand and go the round
Of many plates with towels many times."

"And what is that? You only put me off."

"Rank weeds that love the water from the dishpan
More than some women like the dishpan, Joe;
A little stretch of mowing-field for you;
Not much of that until I come to woods
That end all. And it's scarce enough to call
A view."

          "And yet you think you like it, dear?"

"That's what you're so concerned to know! You hope
I like it. Bang goes something big away
Off there upstairs. The very tread of men
As great as those is shattering to the frame
Of such a little house. Once left alone,
You and I, dear, will go with softer steps
Up and down stairs and through the rooms, and none
But sudden winds that snatch them from our hands
Will ever slam the doors."

                    "I think you see
More than you like to own to out that window."

"No; for beside the things I tell you of,
I only see the years. They come and go
In alternation with the weeds, the field,
The wood."

          "What kind of years?"

                         "Why, latter years—
Different from early years."

— 170—

      "I see them, too.
You didn't count them?"

       "No, the further off
So ran together that I didn't try to.
It can scarce be that they would be in number
We'd care to know, for we are not young now.
And bang goes something else away off there.
It sounds as if it were the men went down,
And every crash meant one less to return
To lighted city streets we, too, have known,
But now are giving up for country darkness."

"Come from that window where you see too much
  for me,
And take a livelier view of things from here.
They're going. Watch this husky swarming up
Over the wheel into the sky-high seat,
Lighting his pipe now, squinting down his nose
At the flame burning downward as he sucks it."

"See how it makes his nose-side bright, a proof
How dark it's getting. Can you tell what time
It is by that? Or by the moon? The new moon!
What shoulder did I see her over? Neither.
A wire she is of silver, as new as we
To everything. Her light won't last us long.
It's something, though, to know we're going to have her
Night after night and stronger every night
To see us through our first two weeks. But, Joe,
The stove! Before they go! Knock on the window;
Ask them to help you get it on its feet.
We stand here dreaming. Hurry! Call them back!"

"They're not gone yet."

      "We've got to have the stove,
Whatever else we want for. And a light.

Have we a piece of candle if the lamp
And oil are buried out of reach?"

                                        Again
The house was full of tramping, and the dark,
Door-filling men burst in and seized the stove.
A cannon-mouth-like hole was in the wall,
To which they set it true by eye; and then
Came up the jointed stovepipe in their hands,
So much too light and airy for their strength
It almost seemed to come ballooning up,
Slipping from clumsy clutches toward the ceiling.
"A fit!" said one, and banged a stovepipe shoulder.
"It's good luck when you move in to begin
With good luck with your stovepipe. Never mind,
It's not so bad in the country, settled down,
When people're getting on in life. You'll like it."

Joe said: "You big boys ought to find a farm,
And make good farmers, and leave other fellows
The city work to do. There's not enough
For everybody as it is in there."

"God!" one said wildly, and, when no one spoke:
"Say that to Jimmy here. He needs a farm."
But Jimmy only made his jaw recede
Fool-like, and rolled his eyes as if to say
He saw himself a farmer. Then there was a French boy
Who said with seriousness that made them laugh,
"Ma friend, you ain't know what it is you're ask."
He doffed his cap and held it with both hands
Across his chest to make as 'twere a bow:
"We're giving you our chances on de farm."
And then they all turned to with deafening boots
And put each other bodily out of the house.

"Goodby to them! We puzzle them. They think—
I don't know what they think we see in what
They leave us to: that pasture slope that seems
The back some farm presents us; and your woods
To northward from your window at the sink,
Waiting to steal a step on us whenever
We drop our eyes or turn to other things,
As in the game 'Ten-step' the children play."

"Good boys they seemed, and let them love the city.
All they could say was 'God!' when you proposed
Their coming out and making useful farmers."

"Did they make something lonesome go through you?
It would take more than them to sicken you—
Us of our bargain. But they left us so
As to our fate, like fools past reasoning with.
They almost shook *me*."

                 "It's all so much
What we have always wanted, I confess
It's seeming bad for a moment makes it seem
Even worse still, and so on down, down, down.
It's nothing; it's their leaving us at dusk.
I never bore it well when people went.
The first night after guests have gone, the house
Seems haunted or exposed. I always take
A personal interest in the locking up
At bedtime; but the strangeness soon wears off."
He fetched a dingy lantern from behind
A door. "There's that we didn't lose! And these!"—
Some matches he unpocketed. "For food—
The meals we've had no one can take from us.
I wish that everything on earth were just
As certain as the meals we've had. I wish
The meals we haven't had were, anyway.
What have you you know where to lay your hands on?"

"The bread we bought in passing at the store.
There's butter somewhere, too."

                                        "Let's rend the bread.
I'll light the fire for company for you;
You'll not have any other company
Till Ed begins to get out on a Sunday
To look us over and give us his idea
Of what wants pruning, shingling, breaking up.
He'll know what he would do if he were we,
And all at once. He'll plan for us and plan
To help us, but he'll take it out in planning.
Well, you can set the table with the loaf.
Let's see you find your loaf. I'll light the fire.
I like chairs occupying other chairs
Not offering a lady——"

                                        "There again, Joe!
You're tired."

                    "I'm drunk-nonsensical tired out;
Don't mind a word I say. It's a day's work
To empty one house of all household goods
And fill another with 'em fifteen miles away,
Although you do no more than dump them down."

"Dumped down in paradise we are and happy."

"It's all so much what I have always wanted,
I can't believe it's what you wanted, too."

"Shouldn't you like to know?"

                                        "I'd like to know
If it is what you wanted, then how much
You wanted it for me."

"A troubled conscience!
You don't want me to tell if *I* don't know."

"I don't want to find out what can't be known.
But who first said the word to come?"

                              "My dear,
It's who first thought the thought. You're searching, Joe,
For things that don't exist; I mean beginnings.
Ends and beginnings—there are no such things.
There are only middles."

                    "What is this?"

                              "This life?
Our sitting here by lantern-light together
Amid the wreckage of a former home?
You won't deny the lantern isn't new.
The stove is not, and you are not to me,
Nor I to you."

               "Perhaps you never were?"

"It would take me forever to recite
All that's not new in where we find ourselves.
New is a word for fools in towns who think
Style upon style in dress and thought at last
Must get somewhere. I've heard you say as much.
No, this is no beginning."

                    "Then an end?"

"End is a gloomy word."

               "Is it too late
To drag you out for just a good-night call

On the old peach trees on the knoll to grope
By starlight in the grass for a last peach
The neighbors may not have taken as their right
When the house wasn't lived in? I've been looking:
I doubt if they have left us many grapes.
Before we set ourselves to right the house,
The first thing in the morning, out we go
To go the round of apple, cherry, peach,
Pine, alder, pasture, mowing, well, and brook.
All of a farm it is."

       "I know this much:
I'm going to put you in your bed, if first
I have to make you build it. Come, the light."

When there was no more lantern in the kitchen,
The fire got out through crannies in the stove
And danced in yellow wrigglers on the ceiling,
As much at home as if they'd always danced there.

THE TELEPHONE

"When I was just as far as I could walk
From here today,
There was an hour
All still
When leaning with my head against a flower
I heard you talk.
Don't say I didn't, for I heard you say—
You spoke from that flower on the window sill—
Do you remember what it was you said?"

"First tell me what it was you thought you heard."

"Having found the flower and driven a bee away,
I leaned my head,
And holding by the stalk,
I listened and I thought I caught the word—
What was it? Did you call me by my name?
Or did you say—
Someone said 'Come'—I heard it as I bowed."

"I may have thought as much, but not aloud."

"Well, so I came."

MEETING AND PASSING

As I went down the hill along the wall
There was a gate I had leaned at for the view
And had just turned from when I first saw you
As you came up the hill. We met. But all
We did that day was mingle great and small
Footprints in summer dust as if we drew
The figure of our being less than two
But more than one as yet. Your parasol
Pointed the decimal off with one deep thrust.
And all the time we talked you seemed to see
Something down there to smile at in the dust.
(Oh, it was without prejudice to me!)
Afterward I went past what you had passed
Before we met and you what I had passed.

HYLA BROOK

By June our brook's run out of song and speed.
Sought for much after that, it will be found
Either to have gone groping underground
(And taken with it all the Hyla breed
That shouted in the mist a month ago,
Like ghost of sleigh bells in a ghost of snow)—
Or flourished and come up in jewelweed,
Weak foliage that is blown upon and bent
Even against the way its waters went.
Its bed is left a faded paper sheet
Of dead leaves stuck together by the heat—
A brook to none but who remember long.
This as it will be seen is other far
Than with brooks taken otherwhere in song.
We love the things we love for what they are.

THE OVEN BIRD

There is a singer everyone has heard,
Loud, a midsummer and a mid-wood bird,
Who makes the solid tree trunks sound again.
He says that leaves are old and that for flowers
Midsummer is to spring as one to ten.
He says the early petal-fall is past
When pear and cherry bloom went down in showers
On sunny days a moment overcast;
And comes that other fall we name the fall.
He says the highway dust is over all.
The bird would cease and be as other birds
But that he knows in singing not to sing.
The question that he frames in all but words
Is what to make of a diminished thing.

BOND AND FREE

Love has earth to which she clings
With hills and circling arms about—
Wall within wall to shut fear out.
But Thought has need of no such things,
For Thought has a pair of dauntless wings.

On snow and sand and turf, I see
Where Love has left a printed trace
With straining in the world's embrace.
And such is Love and glad to be.
But Thought has shaken his ankles free.

Thought cleaves the interstellar gloom
And sits in Sirius' disc all night,
Till day makes him retrace his flight,
With smell of burning on every plume,
Back past the sun to an earthly room.

His gains in heaven are what they are.
Yet some say Love by being thrall
And simply staying possesses all
In several beauty that Thought fares far
To find fused in another star.

BIRCHES

When I see birches bend to left and right
Across the lines of straighter darker trees,
I like to think some boy's been swinging them.
But swinging doesn't bend them down to stay.
Icestorms do that. Often you must have seen them
Loaded with ice a sunny winter morning
After a rain. They click upon themselves
As the breeze rises, and turn many-colored
As the stir cracks and crazes their enamel.
Soon the sun's warmth makes them shed crystal shells
Shattering and avalanching on the snow-crust—
Such heaps of broken glass to sweep away
You'd think the inner dome of heaven had fallen.
They are dragged to the withered bracken by the load,
And they seem not to break; though once they are bowed
So low for long, they never right themselves:
You may see their trunks arching in the woods
Years afterwards, trailing their leaves on the ground
Like girls on hands and knees that throw their hair
Before them over their heads to dry in the sun.
But I was going to say when Truth broke in
With all her matter-of-fact about the icestorm
(Now am I free to be poetical?)
I should prefer to have some boy bend them
As he went out and in to fetch the cows—
Some boy too far from town to learn baseball,
Whose only play was what he found himself,
Summer or winter, and could play alone.
One by one he subdued his father's trees
By riding them down over and over again
Until he took the stiffness out of them,

And not one but hung limp, not one was left
For him to conquer. He learned all there was
To learn about not launching out too soon
And so not carrying the tree away
Clear to the ground. He always kept his poise
To the top branches, climbing carefully
With the same pains you use to fill a cup
Up to the brim, and even above the brim.
Then he flung outward, feet first, with a swish,
Kicking his way down through the air to the ground.
So was I once myself a swinger of birches.
And so I dream of going back to be.
It's when I'm weary of considerations,
And life is too much like a pathless wood
Where your face burns and tickles with the cobwebs
Broken across it, and one eye is weeping
From a twig's having lashed across it open.
I'd like to get away from earth awhile
And then come back to it and begin over.
May no fate willfully misunderstand me
And half grant what I wish and snatch me away
Not to return. Earth's the right place for love:
I don't know where it's likely to go better.
I'd like to go by climbing a birch tree,
And climb black branches up a snow-white trunk
Toward heaven, till the tree could bear no more,
But dipped its top and set me down again.
That would be good both going and coming back.
One could do worse than be a swinger of birches.

PEA BRUSH

I walked down alone Sunday after church
   To the place where John has been cutting trees
To see for myself about the birch
   He said I could have to bush my peas.

The sun in the new-cut narrow gap
   Was hot enough for the first of May,
And stifling hot with the odor of sap
   From stumps still bleeding their life away.

The frogs that were peeping a thousand shrill
   Wherever the ground was low and wet,
The minute they heard my step went still
   To watch me and see what I came to get.

Birch boughs enough piled everywhere!—
   All fresh and sound from the recent axe.
Time someone came with cart and pair
   And got them off the wild flower's backs.

They might be good for garden things
   To curl a little finger round,
The same as you seize cat's-cradle strings,
   And lift themselves up off the ground.

Small good to anything growing wild,
   They were crooking many a trillium
That had budded before the boughs were piled
   And since it was coming up had to come.

PUTTING IN THE SEED

You come to fetch me from my work tonight
When supper's on the table, and we'll see
If I can leave off burying the white
Soft petals fallen from the apple tree.

(Soft petals, yes, but not so barren quite,
Mingled with these, smooth bean and wrinkled pea;)
And go along with you ere you lose sight
Of what you came for and become like me,

Slave to a springtime passion for the earth.
How Love burns through the Putting in the Seed
On through the watching for that early birth
When, just as the soil tarnishes with weed,

The sturdy seedling with arched body comes
Shouldering its way and shedding the earth crumbs.

A TIME TO TALK

When a friend calls to me from the road
And slows his horse to a meaning walk,
I don't stand still and look around
On all the hills I haven't hoed,
And shout from where I am, What is it?
No, not as there is a time to talk.
I thrust my hoe in the mellow ground,
Blade-end up and five feet tall,
And plod: I go up to the stone wall
For a friendly visit.

THE COW IN APPLE TIME

Something inspires the only cow of late
To make no more of a wall than an open gate,
And think no more of wall-builders than fools.
Her face is flecked with pomace and she drools
A cider syrup. Having tasted fruit,
She scorns a pasture withering to the root.
She runs from tree to tree where lie and sweeten
The windfalls spiked with stubble and worm-eaten.
She leaves them bitten when she has to fly.
She bellows on a knoll against the sky.
Her udder shrivels and the milk goes dry.

AN ENCOUNTER

Once on the kind of day called "weather breeder,"
When the heat slowly hazes and the sun
By its own power seems to be undone,
I was half boring through, half climbing through
A swamp of cedar. Choked with oil of cedar
And scurf of plants, and weary and overheated,
And sorry I ever left the road I knew,
I paused and rested on a sort of hook
That had me by the coat as good as seated,
And since there was no other way to look,
Looked up toward heaven, and there against the blue,
Stood over me a resurrected tree,
A tree that had been down and raised again—
A barkless spectre. He had halted too,
As if for fear of treading upon me.
I saw the strange position of his hands—
Up at his shoulders, dragging yellow strands
Of wire with something in it from men to men.
"You here?" I said. "Where aren't you nowadays
And what's the news you carry—if you know?
And tell me where you're off for—Montreal?
Me? I'm not off for anywhere at all.
Sometimes I wander out of beaten ways
Half looking for the orchid Calypso."

RANGE-FINDING

The battle rent a cobweb diamond-strung
And cut a flower beside a ground bird's nest
Before it stained a single human breast.
The stricken flower bent double and so hung.
And still the bird revisited her young.
A butterfly its fall had dispossessed
A moment sought in air his flower of rest,
Then lightly stooped to it and fluttering clung.

On the bare upland pasture there had spread
O'ernight 'twixt mullein stalks a wheel of thread
And straining cables wet with silver dew.
A sudden passing bullet shook it dry.
The indwelling spider ran to greet the fly,
But finding nothing, sullenly withdrew.

THE HILL WIFE

LONELINESS

(Her Word)

One ought not to have to care
   So much as you and I
Care when the birds come round the house
   To seem to say good-bye;

Or care so much when they come back
   With whatever it is they sing;
The truth being we are as much
   Too glad for the one thing

As we are too sad for the other here—
   With birds that fill their breasts
But with each other and themselves
   And their built or driven nests.

HOUSE FEAR

Always—I tell you this they learned—
Always at night when they returned
To the lonely house from far away
To lamps unlighted and fire gone gray,
They learned to rattle the lock and key
To give whatever might chance to be
Warning and time to be off in flight:
And preferring the out- to the in-door night,
They learned to leave the house-door wide
Until they had lit the lamp inside.

THE SMILE
(Her Word)

I didn't like the way he went away.
That smile! It never came of being gay.
Still he smiled—did you see him?—I was
    sure!
Perhaps because we gave him only bread
And the wretch knew from that that we
    were poor.
Perhaps because he let us give instead
Of seizing from us as he might have seized.
Perhaps he mocked at us for being wed,
Or being very young (and he was pleased
To have a vision of us old and dead).
I wonder how far down the road he's got.
He's watching from the woods as like as
    not.

THE OFT-REPEATED DREAM

She had no saying dark enough
   For the dark pine that kept
Forever trying the window-latch
   Of the room where they slept.

The tireless but ineffectual hands
   That with every futile pass
Made the great tree seem as a little bird
   Before the mystery of glass!

It never had been inside the room,
   And only one of the two
Was afraid in an oft-repeated dream
   Of what the tree might do.

It was too lonely for her there,
   And too wild,
And since there were but two of them,
   And no child,

And work was little in the house,
   She was free,
And followed where he furrowed field,
   Or felled tree.

She rested on a log and tossed
   The fresh chips,
With a song only to herself
   On her lips.

And once she went to break a bough
   Of black alder.
She strayed so far she scarcely heard
   When he called her—

And didn't answer—didn't speak—
   Or return.
She stood, and then she ran and hid
   In the fern.

He never found her, though he looked
   Everywhere,
And he asked at her mother's house
   Was she there.

Sudden and swift and light as that
   The ties gave,
And he learned of finalities
   Besides the grave.

THE BONFIRE

"Oh, let's go up the hill and scare ourselves,
As reckless as the best of them tonight,
By setting fire to all the brush we piled
With pitchy hands to wait for rain or snow.
Oh, let's not wait for rain to make it safe.
The pile is ours: we dragged it bough on bough
Down dark converging paths between the pines.
Let's not care what we do with it tonight.
Divide it? No! But burn it as one pile
The way we piled it. And let's be the talk
Of people brought to windows by a light
Thrown from somewhere against their wallpaper.
Rouse them all, both the free and not so free
With saying what they'd like to do to us
For what they'd better wait till we have done.
Let's all but bring to life this old volcano,
If that is what the mountain ever was—
And scare ourselves. Let wild fire loose we will. . . ."
"And scare you too?" the children said together.

"Why wouldn't it scare me to have a fire
Begin in smudge with ropy smoke and know
That still, if I repent, I may recall it,
But in a moment not: a little spurt
Of burning fatness, and then nothing but
The fire itself can put it out, and that
By burning out, and before it burns out
It will have roared first and mixed sparks with stars,
And sweeping round it with a flaming sword,
Made the dim trees stand back in wider circle—
Done so much and I know not how much more

I mean it shall not do if I can bind it.
Well if it doesn't with its draft bring on
A wind to blow in earnest from some quarter,
As once it did with me upon an April.
The breezes were so spent with winter blowing
They seemed to fail the bluebirds under them
Short of the perch their languid flight was toward;
And my flame made a pinnacle to heaven
As I walked once round it in possession.
But the wind out of doors—you know the saying.
There came a gust. You used to think the trees
Made wind by fanning since you never knew
It blow but that you saw the trees in motion.
Something or someone watching made that gust.
It put that flame tip-down and dabbed the grass
Of over-winter with the least tip-touch
Your tongue gives salt or sugar in your hand.
The place it reached to blackened instantly.
The black was all there was by daylight,
That and the merest curl of cigarette smoke—
And a flame slender as the hepaticas,
Blood-root, and violets so soon to be now.
But the black spread like black death on the ground,
And I think the sky darkened with a cloud
Like winter and evening coming on together.
There were enough things to be thought of then.
Where the field stretches toward the north
And setting sun to Hyla brook, I gave it
To flames without twice thinking, where it verges
Upon the road, to flames too, though in fear
They might find fuel there, in withered brake,
Grass its full length, old silver goldenrod,
And alder and grape vine entanglement,
To leap the dusty deadline. For my own
I took what front there was beside. I knelt
And thrust hands in and held my face away.

Fight such a fire by rubbing not by beating.
A board is the best weapon if you have it.
I had my coat. And oh, I knew, I knew,
And said out loud, I couldn't bide the smother
And heat so close in; but the thought of all
The woods and town on fire by me, and all
The town turned out to fight for me—that held me.
I trusted the brook barrier, but feared
The road would fail; and on that side the fire
Died not without a noise of crackling wood—
Of something more than tinder-grass and weed—
That brought me to my feet to hold it back
By leaning back myself, as if the reins
Were round my neck and I was at the plough.
I won! But I'm sure no one ever spread
Another color over a tenth the space
That I spread coal-black over in the time
It took me. Neighbors coming home from town
Couldn't believe that so much black had come there
While they had backs turned, that it hadn't been there
When they had passed an hour or so before
Going the other way and they not seen it.
They looked about for someone to have done it.
But there was no one. I was somewhere wondering
Where all my weariness had gone and why
I walked so light on air in heavy shoes
In spite of a scorched Fourth-of-July feeling.
Why wouldn't I be scared remembering that?"

"If it scares you, what will it do to us?"

"Scare you. But if you shrink from being scared,
What would you say to war if it should come?
That's what for reasons I should like to know—
If you can comfort me by any answer."

"Oh, but war's not for children—it's for men."

"Now we are digging almost down to China.
My dears, my dears, you thought that—we all thought it.
So your mistake was ours. Haven't you heard, though,
About the ships where war has found them out
At sea, about the towns where war has come
Through opening clouds at night with droning speed
Further o'erhead than all but stars and angels,—
And children in the ships and in the towns?
Haven't you heard what we have lived to learn?
Nothing so new—something we had forgotten:
War is for everyone, for children too.
I wasn't going to tell you and I mustn't.
The best way is to come up hill with me
And have our fire and laugh and be afraid."

A GIRL'S GARDEN

A neighbor of mine in the village
    Likes to tell how one spring
When she was a girl on the farm, she did
    A childlike thing.

One day she asked her father
    To give her a garden plot
To plant and tend and reap herself,
    And he said, "Why not?"

In casting about for a corner
    He thought of an idle bit
Of walled-off ground where a shop had stood,
    And he said, "Just it."

And he said, "That ought to make you
    An ideal one-girl farm,
And give you a chance to put some strength
    On your slim-jim arm."

It was not enough of a garden,
    Her father said, to plough;
So she had to work it all by hand,
    But she don't mind now.

She wheeled the dung in the wheelbarrow
    Along a stretch of road;
But she always ran away and left
    Her not-nice load,

And hid from anyone passing.
    And then she begged the seed.
She says she thinks she planted one
    Of all things but weed.

A hill each of potatoes,
    Radishes, lettuce, peas,
Tomatoes, beets, beans, pumpkins, corn,
    And even fruit trees.

And yes, she has long mistrusted
    That a cider apple tree
In bearing there today is hers,
    Or at least may be.

Her crop was a miscellany
    When all was said and done,
A little bit of everything,
    A great deal of none.

Now when she sees in the village
    How village things go,
Just when it seems to come in right,
    She says, "*I* know!

It's as when I was a farmer——"
    Oh, never by way of advice!
And she never sins by telling the tale
    To the same person twice.

THE EXPOSED NEST

You were forever finding some new play.
So when I saw you down on hands and knees
In the meadow, busy with the new-cut hay,
Trying, I thought, to set it up on end,
I went to show you how to make it stay,
If that was your idea, against the breeze,
And, if you asked me, even help pretend
To make it root again and grow afresh.
But 'twas no make-believe with you today,
Nor was the grass itself your real concern,
Though I found your hand full of wilted fern,
Steel-bright June-grass, and blackening heads of clover.
'Twas a nest full of young birds on the ground
The cutter-bar had just gone champing over
(Miraculously without tasting flesh)
And left defenseless to the heat and light.
You wanted to restore them to their right
Of something interposed between their sight
And too much world at once—could means be found.
The way the nest-full every time we stirred
Stood up to us as to a mother-bird
Whose coming home has been too long deferred,
Made me ask would the mother-bird return
And care for them in such a change of scene
And might our meddling make her more afraid.
That was a thing we could not wait to learn.
We saw the risk we took in doing good,
But dared not spare to do the best we could
Though harm should come of it; so built the screen
You had begun, and gave them back their shade.

All this to prove we cared. Why is there then
No more to tell? We turned to other things.
I haven't any memory—have you?—
Of ever coming to the place again
To see if the birds lived the first night through,
And so at last to learn to use their wings.

"OUT, OUT—"

The buzz-saw snarled and rattled in the yard
And made dust and dropped stove-length sticks of
        wood,
Sweet-scented stuff when the breeze drew across it.
And from there those that lifted eyes could count
Five mountain ranges one behind the other
Under the sunset far into Vermont.
And the saw snarled and rattled, snarled and rattled,
As it ran light, or had to bear a load.
And nothing happened: day was all but done.
Call it a day, I wish they might have said
To please the boy by giving him the half hour
That a boy counts so much when saved from work.
His sister stood beside them in her apron
To tell them "Supper." At that word, the saw,
As if to prove saws knew what supper meant,
Leaped out at the boy's hand, or seemed to leap—
He must have given the hand. However it was,
Neither refused the meeting. But the hand!
The boy's first outcry was a rueful laugh,
As he swung toward them holding up the hand
Half in appeal, but half as if to keep
The life from spilling. Then the boy saw all—
Since he was old enough to know, big boy
Doing a man's work, though a child at heart—
He saw all spoiled. "Don't let him cut my hand off—
The doctor, when he comes. Don't let him, sister!"

So. But the hand was gone already.
The doctor put him in the dark of ether.
He lay and puffed his lips out with his breath.
And then—the watcher at his pulse took fright.
No one believed. They listened at his heart.
Little—less—nothing!—and that ended it.
No more to build on there. And they, since they
Were not the one dead, turned to their affairs.

BROWN'S DESCENT

OR

THE WILLY-NILLY SLIDE

Brown lived at such a lofty farm
   That everyone for miles could see
His lantern when he did his chores
   In winter after half past three.

And many must have seen him make
   His wild descent from there one night,
'Cross lots, 'cross walls, 'cross everything,
   Describing rings of lantern light.

Between the house and barn the gale
   Got him by something he had on
And blew him out on the icy crust
   That cased the world, and he was gone!

Walls were all buried, trees were few:
   He saw no stay unless he stove
A hole in somewhere with his heel.
   But though repeatedly he strove

And stamped and said things to himself,
   And sometimes something seemed to yield.
He gained no foothold, but pursued
   His journey down from field to field.

Sometimes he came with arms outspread
   Like wings, revolving in the scene
Upon his longer axis, and
   With no small dignity of mien.

Faster or slower as he chanced,
    Sitting or standing as he chose,
According as he feared to risk
    His neck, or thought to spare his clothes.

He never let the lantern drop.
    And some exclaimed who saw afar
The figures he described with it,
    "I wonder what those signals are

Brown makes at such an hour of night!
    He's celebrating something strange.
I wonder if he's sold his farm,
    Or been made Master of the Grange."

He reeled, he lurched, he bobbed, he checked;
    He fell and made the lantern rattle
(But saved the light from going out.)
    So halfway down he fought the battle

Incredulous of his own bad luck.
    And then becoming reconciled
To everything, he gave it up
    And came down like a coasting child.

"Well—I—be—" that was all he said,
    As standing in the river road,
He looked back up the slippery slope
    (Two miles it was) to his abode.

Sometimes as an authority
    On motorcars, I'm asked if I
Should say our stock was petered out,
    And this is my sincere reply:

Yankees are what they always were.
    Don't think Brown ever gave up hope
Of getting home again because
    He couldn't climb that slippery slope;

Or even thought of standing there
    Until the January thaw
Should take the polish off the crust.
    He bowed with grace to natural law,

And then went round it on his feet,
    After the manner of our stock;
Not much concerned for those to whom,
    At that particular time o'clock,

It must have looked as if the course
    He steered was really straight away
From that which he was headed for—
    Not much concerned for them, I say;

No more so than became a man—
    And politician at odd seasons.
I've kept Brown standing in the cold
    While I invested him with reasons;

But now he snapped his eyes three times;
    Then shook his lantern saying, "Ile's
'Bout out!" and took the long way home
    By road, a matter of several miles.

THE GUM-GATHERER

There overtook me and drew me in
To his down-hill, early-morning stride,
And set me five miles on my road
Better than if he had had me ride,
A man with a swinging bag for load
And half the bag wound round his hand.
We talked like barking above the din
Of water we walked along beside.
And for my telling him where I'd been
And where I lived in mountain land
To be coming home the way I was,
He told me a little about himself.
He came from higher up in the pass
Where the grist of the new-beginning brooks
Is blocks split off the mountain mass—
And hopeless grist enough it looks
Ever to grind to soil for grass.
(The way it is will do for moss.)
There he had built his stolen shack.
It had to be a stolen shack
Because of the fears of fire and loss
That trouble the sleep of lumber folk:
Visions of half the world burned black
And the sun shrunken yellow in smoke.
We know who when they come to town
Bring berries under the wagon seat,
Or a basket of eggs between their feet;
What this man brought in a cotton sack
Was gum, the gum of the mountain spruce.

He showed me lumps of the scented stuff
Like uncut jewels, dull and rough.
It comes to market golden brown;
But turns to pink between the teeth.

I told him this is a pleasant life
To set your breast to the bark of trees
That all your days are dim beneath,
And reaching up with a little knife,
To loose the resin and take it down
And bring it to market when you please.

THE LINE-GANG

Here come the line-gang pioneering by.
They throw a forest down less cut than broken.
They plant dead trees for living, and the dead
They string together with a living thread.
They string an instrument against the sky
Wherein words whether beaten out or spoken
Will run as hushed as when they were a thought.
But in no hush they string it: they go past
With shouts afar to pull the cable taut,
To hold it hard until they make it fast,
To ease away—they have it. With a laugh,
An oath of towns that set the wild at naught
They bring the telephone and telegraph.

THE VANISHING RED

He is said to have been the last Red Man
In Acton. And the Miller is said to have laughed—
If you like to call such a sound a laugh.
But he gave no one else a laughter's license.
For he turned suddenly grave as if to say,
"Whose business,—if I take it on myself,
Whose business—but why talk round the barn?—
When it's just that I hold with getting a thing done with."

You can't get back and see it as he saw it.
It's too long a story to go into now.
You'd have to have been there and lived it.
Then you wouldn't have looked on it as just a matter
Of who began it between the two races.

Some guttural exclamation of surprise
The Red Man gave in poking about the mill
Over the great big thumping shuffling millstone
Disgusted the Miller physically as coming
From one who had no right to be heard from.

"Come, John," he said, "you want to see the wheel pit?"

He took him down below a cramping rafter,
And showed him, through a manhole in the floor,
The water in desperate straits like frantic fish,
Salmon and sturgeon, lashing with their tails.
Then he shut down the trap door with a ring in it
That jangled even above the general noise,
And came up stairs alone—and gave that laugh,
And said something to a man with a meal-sack
That the man with the meal-sack didn't catch—then.
Oh, yes, he showed John the wheel pit all right.

SNOW

The three stood listening to a fresh access
Of wind that caught against the house a moment,
Gulped snow, and then blew free again—the Coles
Dressed, but dishevelled from some hours of sleep,
Meserve belittled in the great skin coat he wore.

Meserve was first to speak. He pointed backward
Over his shoulder with his pipe-stem, saying,
"You can just see it glancing off the roof
Making a great scroll upward toward the sky,
Long enough for recording all our names on.—
I think I'll just call up my wife and tell her
I'm here—so far—and starting on again.
I'll call her softly so that if she's wise
And gone to sleep, she needn't wake to answer."
Three times he barely stirred the bell, then listened.
"Why, Lett, still up? Lett, I'm at Cole's. I'm late.
I called you up to say Good night from here
Before I went to say Good morning there.—
I thought I would.—I know, but, Lett—I know—
I could, but what's the sense? The rest won't be
So bad.—Give me an hour for it.—Ho, ho,
Three hours to here! But that was all up hill;
The rest is down.—Why no, no, not a wallow:
They kept their heads and took their time to it
Like darlings, both of them. They're in the barn.—
My dear, I'm coming just the same. I didn't
Call you to ask you to invite me home.—"

He lingered for some word she wouldn't say,
Said it at last himself, "Good night," and then,

Getting no answer, closed the telephone.
The three stood in the lamplight round the table
With lowered eyes a moment till he said,
"I'll just see how the horses are."

                              "Yes, do,"
Both the Coles said together. Mrs. Cole
Added: "You can judge better after seeing.—
I want you here with me, Fred. Leave him here,
Brother Meserve. You know to find your way
Out through the shed."

                              "I guess I know my way,
I guess I know where I can find my name
Carved in the shed to tell me who I am
If it don't tell me where I am. I used
To play—"

                    "You tend your horses and come back.
Fred Cole, you're going to let him!"

                                        "Well, aren't you?
How can you help yourself?"

                                    "I called him Brother.
Why did I call him that?"

                              "It's right enough.
That's all you ever heard him called round here.
He seems to have lost off his Christian name."

"Christian enough I should call that myself.
He took no notice, did he? Well, at least
I didn't use it out of love of him,
The dear knows. I detest the thought of him
With his ten children under ten years old.

I hate his wretched little Racker Sect,
All's ever I heard of it, which isn't much.
But that's not saying—Look, Fred Cole, it's twelve,
Isn't it, now? He's been here half an hour.
He says he left the village store at nine.
Three hours to do four miles—a mile an hour
Or not much better. Why, it doesn't seem
As if a man could move that slow and move.
Try to think what he did with all that time.
And three miles more to go!"

                              "Don't let him go.
Stick to him, Helen. Make him answer you.
That sort of man talks straight on all his life
From the last thing he said himself, stone deaf
To anything anyone else may say.
I should have thought, though, you could make him
        hear you."

"What is he doing out a night like this?
Why can't he stay at home?"

                              "He had to preach."

"It's no night to be out."

                              "He may be small,
He may be good, but one thing's sure, he's tough."

"And strong of stale tobacco."

                              "He'll pull through."

"You only say so. Not another house
Or shelter to put into from this place
To theirs. I'm going to call his wife again."

"Wait and he may. Let's see what he will do.
Let's see if he will think of her again.
But then I doubt he's thinking of himself
He doesn't look on it as anything."

"He shan't go—there!"

                         "It *is* a night, my dear."

"One thing: he didn't drag God into it."

"He don't consider it a case for God."

"You think so, do you? You don't know the kind.
He's getting up a miracle this minute.
Privately—to himself, right now, he's thinking
He'll make a case of it if he succeeds,
But keep still if he fails."

                    "Keep still all over.
He'll be dead—dead and buried."

                              "Such a trouble!
Not but I've every reason not to care
What happens to him if it only takes
Some of the sanctimonious conceit
Out of one of those pious scalawags."

"Nonsense to that! You want to see him safe."

"You like the runt."

                "Don't you a little?"

                                   "Well,
I don't like what he's doing, which is what
You like, and like him for."

                              "Oh, yes you do.
You like your fun as well as anyone;
Only you women have to put these airs on
To impress men. You've got us so ashamed
Of being men we can't look at a good fight
Between two boys and not feel bound to stop it.
Let the man freeze an ear or two, I say.—
He's here. I leave him all to you. Go in
And save his life.—All right, come in, Meserve.
Sit down, sit down. How did you find the horses?"

"Fine, fine."

"And ready for some more? My wife here
Says it won't do. You've got to give it up."

"Won't you to please me? Please! If I say please?
Mr. Meserve, I'll leave it to *your* wife.
What *did* your wife say on the telephone?"

Meserve seemed to heed nothing but the lamp
Or something not far from it on the table.
By straightening out and lifting a forefinger,
He pointed with his hand from where it lay
Like a white crumpled spider on his knee:
"That leaf there in your open book! It moved
Just then, I thought. It stood erect like that,
There on the table, ever since I came,
Trying to turn itself backward or forward,
I've had my eye on it to make out which;
If forward, then it's with a friend's impatience—
You see I know—to get you on to things
It wants to see how you will take, if backward
It's from regret for something you have passed
And failed to see the good of. Never mind,

Things must expect to come in front of us
A many times—I don't say just how many—
That varies with the things—before we see them.
One of the lies would make it out that nothing
Ever presents itself before us twice.
Where would we be at last if that were so?
Our very life depends on everything's
Recurring till we answer from within.
The thousandth time may prove the charm.—That leaf!
It can't turn either way. It needs the wind's help.
But the wind didn't move it if it moved.
It moved itself. The wind's at naught in here.
It couldn't stir so sensitively poised
A thing as that. It couldn't reach the lamp
To get a puff of black smoke from the flame,
Or blow a rumple in the collie's coat.
You make a little foursquare block of air,
Quiet and light and warm, in spite of all
The illimitable dark and cold and storm,
And by so doing give these three, lamp, dog,
And book-leaf, that keep near you, their repose;
Though for all anyone can tell, repose
May be the thing you haven't, yet you give it.
So false it is that what we haven't we can't give;
So false, that what we always say is true.
I'll have to turn the leaf if no one else will.
It won't lie down. Then let it stand. Who cares?"

"I shouldn't want to hurry you, Meserve,
But if you're going—Say you'll stay, you know?
But let me raise this curtain on a scene,
And show you how it's piling up against you.
You see the snow-white through the white of frost?
Ask Helen how far up the sash it's climbed
Since last we read the gage."

"It looks as if
Some pallid thing had squashed its features flat
And its eyes shut with overeagerness
To see what people found so interesting
In one another, and had gone to sleep
Of its own stupid lack of understanding,
Or broken its white neck of mushroom stuff
Short off, and died against the windowpane."

"Brother Meserve, take care, you'll scare yourself
More than you will us with such nightmare talk.
It's you it matters to, because it's you
Who have to go out into it alone."

"Let him talk, Helen, and perhaps he'll stay."

"Before you drop the curtain—I'm reminded:
You recollect the boy who came out here
To breathe the air one winter—had a room
Down at the Averys'? Well, one sunny morning
After a downy storm, he passed our place
And found me banking up the house with snow.
And I was burrowing in deep for warmth,
Piling it well above the windowsills.
The snow against the window caught his eye.
'Hey, that's a pretty thought'—those were his words.
'So you can think it's six feet deep outside,
While you sit warm and read up balanced rations.
You can't get too much winter in the winter.'
Those were his words. And he went home and all
But banked the daylight out of Avery's windows.
Now you and I would go to no such length.
At the same time you can't deny it makes
It not a mite worse, sitting here, we three,
Playing our fancy, to have the snowline run
So high across the pane outside. There where
There is a sort of tunnel in the frost

More like a tunnel than a hole—way down
At the far end of it you see a stir
And quiver like the frayed edge of the drift
Blown in the wind. I *like* that—I like *that.*
Well, now I leave you, people."

                       "Come, Meserve,
We thought you were deciding not to go—
The ways you found to say the praise of comfort
And being where you are. You want to stay."

"I'll own it's cold for such a fall of snow.
This house is frozen brittle, all except
This room you sit in. If you think the wind
Sounds further off, it's not because it's dying;
You're further under in the snow—that's all—
And feel it less. Hear the soft bombs of dust
It bursts against us at the chimney mouth,
And at the eaves. I like it from inside
More than I shall out in it. But the horses
Are rested and it's time to say good night,
And let you get to bed again. Good night,
Sorry I had to break in on your sleep."

"Lucky for you you did. Lucky for you
You had us for a halfway station
To stop at. If you were the kind of man
Paid heed to women, you'd take my advice
And for your family's sake stay where you are.
But what good is my saying it over and over?
You've done more than you had a right to think
You could do—*now.* You know the risk you take
In going on."

                  "Our snowstorms as a rule
Aren't looked on as man-killers, and although
I'd rather be the beast that sleeps the sleep

Under it all, his door sealed up and lost,
Than the man fighting it to keep above it,
Yet think of the small birds at roost and not
In nests. Shall I be counted less than they are?
Their bulk in water would be frozen rock
In no time out tonight. And yet tomorrow
They will come budding boughs from tree to tree
Flirting their wings and saying Chickadee,
As if not knowing what you meant by the word storm."

"But why when no one wants you to go on?
Your wife—she doesn't want you to. We don't,
And you yourself don't want to. Who else is there?"

"Save us from being cornered by a woman.
Well, there's"—She told Fred afterward that in
The pause right there, she thought the dreaded word
Was coming, "God." But no, he only said
"Well, there's—the storm. That says I must go on.
That wants me as a war might if it came.
Ask any man."

                    He threw her that as something
To last her till he got outside the door.
He had Cole with him to the barn to see him off.
When Cole returned he found his wife still standing
Beside the table near the open book,
Not reading it.

                    "Well, what kind of a man
Do you call that?" she said.

                    "He had the gift
Of words, or is it tongues, I ought to say?"

"Was ever such a man for seeing likeness?"

"Or disregarding people's civil questions—
What? We've found out in one hour more about him
Than we had seeing him pass by in the road
A thousand times. If that's the way he preaches!
You didn't think you'd keep him after all.
Oh, I'm not blaming you. He didn't leave you
Much say in the matter, and I'm just as glad
We're not in for a night of him. No sleep
If he had stayed. The least thing set him going.
It's quiet as an empty church without him."

"But how much better off are we as it is?
We'll have to sit here till we know he's safe."

"Yes, I suppose you'll want to, but I shouldn't.
He knows what he can do, or he wouldn't try.
Get into bed I say, and get some rest.
He won't come back, and if he telephones,
It won't be for an hour or two."

                                    "Well then.
We can't be any help by sitting here
And living his fight through with him, I suppose."

                    _____

Cole had been telephoning in the dark.

Mrs. Cole's voice came from an inner room:
"Did she call you or you call her?"

                                    "She me.
You'd better dress: you won't go back to bed.
We must have been asleep: it's three and after."

"Had she been ringing long? I'll get my wrapper.
I want to speak to her."

                              "All she said was,
He hadn't come and had he really started."

"She knew he had, poor thing, two hours ago."

"He had the shovel. He'll have made a fight."

"Why did I ever let him leave this house!"

"Don't begin that. You did the best you could
To keep him—though perhaps you didn't quite
Conceal a wish to see him show the spunk
To disobey you. Much his wife'll thank you."

"Fred, after all I said! You shan't make out
That it was any way but what it was.
Did she let on by any word she said
She didn't thank me?"

                              "When I told her 'Gone,'
'Well then,' she said, and 'Well then'—like a threat.
And then her voice came scraping slow: 'Oh, you,
Why did you let him go?' "

                              "Asked why we let him?
You let me there. I'll ask her why she let him.
She didn't dare to speak when he was here.
Their numbers—twenty-one? The thing won't work.
Someone's receiver's down. The handle stumbles.
The stubborn thing, the way it jars your arm!
It's theirs. She's dropped it from her hand and gone."

"Try speaking. Say 'Hello!' "

                              "Hello. Hello."

"What do you hear?"

        "I hear an empty room—
You know—it sounds that way. And yes, I hear—
I think I hear a clock—and windows rattling.
No step though. If she's there she's sitting down."

"Shout, she may hear you."

             "Shouting is no good."

"Keep speaking then."

        "Hello. Hello. Hello.
You don't suppose—? She wouldn't go outdoors?"

"I'm half afraid that's just what she might do."

"And leave the children?"

         "Wait and call again.
You can't hear whether she has left the door
Wide open and the wind's blown out the lamp
And the fire's died and the room's dark and cold?"

"One of two things, either she's gone to bed
Or gone outdoors."

        "In which case both are lost.
Do you know what she's like? Have you ever met her?
It's strange she doesn't want to speak to us."

"Fred, see if you can hear what I hear. Come."

"A clock maybe."

"Don't you hear something else?"

"Not talking."
                    "No."

                    "Why, yes, I hear—what is it?"

"What do you say it is?"

                    "A baby's crying!"

"Frantic it sounds, though muffled and far off."

"Its mother wouldn't let it cry like that,
Not if she's there."

                    "What do you make of it?"

"There's only one thing possible to make,
That is, assuming—that she has gone out.
Of course she hasn't though." They both sat down
Helpless. "There's nothing we can do till morning."

"Fred, I shan't let you think of going out."

"Hold on." The double bell began to chirp.
They started up. Fred took the telephone.
"Hello, Meserve. You're there, then!—And your wife?
Good! Why I asked—she didn't seem to answer.
He says she went to let him in the barn.—
We're glad. Oh, say no more about it, man.
Drop in and see us when you're passing."

                                        "Well,
She has him then, though what she wants him for
I don't see."

                        "Possibly not for herself.
Maybe she only wants him for the children."

"The whole to-do seems to have been for nothing.
What spoiled our night was to him just his fun.
What did he come in for?—To talk and visit?
Thought he'd just call to tell us it was snowing.
If he thinks he is going to make our house
A halfway coffee house 'twixt town and nowhere——"

"I thought you'd feel you'd been too much concerned."

"You think you haven't been concerned yourself."

"If you mean he was inconsiderate
To rout us out to think for him at midnight
And then take our advice no more than nothing,
Why, I agree with you. But let's forgive him.
We've had a share in one night of his life.
What'll you bet he ever calls again?"

THE SOUND OF THE TREES

I wonder about the trees.
Why do we wish to bear
Forever the noise of these
More than another noise
So close to our dwelling place?
We suffer them by the day
Till we lose all measure of pace,
And fixity in our joys,
And acquire a listening air.
They are that that talks of going
But never gets away;
And that talks no less for knowing,
As it grows wiser and older,
That now it means to stay.
My feet tug at the floor
And my head sways to my shoulder
Sometimes when I watch trees sway,
From the window or the door.
I shall set forth for somewhere,
I shall make the reckless choice
Some day when they are in voice
And tossing so as to scare
The white clouds over them on.
I shall have less to say,
But I shall be gone.